KRAMER'S GOATS

Rudolf Nassauer

KRAMER'S GOATS

PETER OWEN · LONDON

ISBN 0 7206 0659 4

PETER OWEN PUBLISHERS
73 Kenway Road London SW5 0RE

First published in Great Britain 1986
© Rudolf Nassauer 1986

Printed in Great Britain by
WBC Print Ltd Barton Manor St Philips Bristol

For Sinclair Beiles

One

On account of Clothilde, my mother's French governess in Vienna, so runs the family yarn, for whatever our mother told us was always tinged, like her face, with make-up, I was named Julien, and my brother, by twelve minutes the younger of us, Fabrizio, adapted to Fabrice to make that silly name more acceptable. Whenever our mother, by crude or subtle means, wished to add spice to some argument to tip it in her favour, she would invoke the spirit of Clothilde who had been engaged by our grandparents to take charge of their only daughter. By the time Maman talked to us about our Viennese past, and hers in particular, and we were old enough to understand, we no longer lived there, so that our view of that city on the banks of the Danube was pure conjecture and, because of Maman's expertise at make-up, embellishment. To be fair, the past is never as true as the present. We know not how to cope with distortion, with the proportions of our nurseries we never had cause to measure, with fading which time inflicts on colours, on smells and pain, so that what we recall is only partially true. This makes us enlarge or diminish the past, invites us to tell white lies about our life, so that our mother's house, we now know, was not as large and elegant as she described it, that there weren't any stables for horses on which they rode in the Wiener Wald, and that no doubt Clothilde was not as stunning as we were made to believe, of such beauty and Parisian chic that men stopped in the street to stare at her as she walked by with her charge. What is true is that she influenced Maman in her reading, and that Stendhal, through her, became Maman's favourite author, which made her choose our names from his two famous heroes.

I have never had any reason to commit myself to paper about Fabrice, and now that I wish to do so I am stumped at what to say, or even where to begin. As you can imagine, it is a most delicate matter for one twin to write about the other, the more so as our genes made us identical. It is, believe me, irritation enough for one of us to be confused with the other, as often happens, at which we have to retreat and point out that we are not the other. These confusions, however, are easy enough to cope with, but not so the delineation between us which makes Fabrice a different person, someone apart from me. We have long learned, my brother and I, to accept proximity, a state between us that exists and would be painful to destroy, but I for one stand guard over my territory and do not allow Fabrice to enter beyond a certain distance. He, I know, does likewise, but he is plagued by the poet's turbulence and flights of imagination which make his frontiers far less stable and secure.

As a bachelor, I sleep on my back and seldom wake in a position other than the one in which I have fallen asleep. I have a sense of inner time, an inborn ability I share with Fabrice, which enables me to wake up each day at seven-fifteen sharp, without the aid of a clock. I become conscious of being awake, but keep my eyes closed. I then half open one eyelid, whichever is the more moist that day, and my first thoughts go out to my burdensome brother. It is, I assure you, not a pleasant connection. I am a calm and fastidious man, whereas my brother is untidy and irregular in his habits, a slave to violent moods and numbness, and spasms of lyrical tranquillity. I go out to him like a lover pursuing his love on the track of obsession and often curse myself for being linked to him. That watchful eye nature decrees for the elder, to hover and protect the younger sibling.

I am a frightened man. Because of my brother's mental state there is no peace in my life. He has suffered innumerable breakdowns over the past fifteen years, and their frequency and severity do not seem to abate. What is more, over the past four years these breakdowns have started to affect my own mental health, and I have had several bouts of illness caused by Fabrice's mad behaviour. I do not know how to escape, which adds further to my state of fright. Fifteen years ago I moved from Johannesburg to London, to escape the stifling clutches of my mother, and two years later my escape was marred when my brother arrived on my doorstep, which was most unfair and inconsiderate. To be fair, and much to my relief, he stayed only a short while, three weeks and two days, before setting off to live abroad for a time. I had obtained, soon after my arrival in London, an excellent job at a museum, where I am in charge of nineteenth-century prints. The director of our section has been most kind and understanding about my health, and has never hinted, let alone suggested, that I should resign my position because of my spells of absence.

I have often thought that my parents should never have moved to South Africa after we left Austria in '38, but refugees are inclined to land anywhere they can gain a foothold. Father was a jeweller with connections in Jo'burg, and that I suppose is why we went there, to a place I have detested as long as I can remember. When Papa died he left me a few thousand pounds, the same as to Fabrice, and whilst Fabrice squandered his little inheritance in a matter of months, I used my part to buy a ticket to London and to purchase a pleasant flat in Earls Court. The flat is sufficient for my needs and has a light, fair-sized room for me to work in, and a pleasant enough room for my bed. I am proficient at looking after myself, and keep the place clean and cook for myself, and occasionally for friends. Simple food. My taste-buds have long lost their yearning for Viennese cooking (that is what my mother called the style of her cuisine), a fact which my analyst finds hard to believe, though I seem finally to have convinced him that refugees can undergo a transmutation so complete that the slate of the past is wiped clean. It was, I suppose, a wilful thing to say to him, and in the end he told me he didn't entirely believe me, and I left it at that because I felt

9

myself to be on shaky ground. I do occasionally slip into a restaurant in the Earls Court Road which serves excellent goulash soup.

My height touches six feet, as does Fabrice's, and both of us are lean, though not overtly so. When I am well my body is strong and my brain functions with a clarity I can best describe as like looking at a landscape after rain. Fabrice once wrote a poem about this. He compared this clarity of mind to the moments before epileptics have their fit, and then he used the image of rain purifying the air so that blades of grass and washed insects become clearly visible. I walk to work most days, but in the evening I can't repeat that four-mile trek and I come home by bus, riding on the top deck. I enjoy walking, but detest hovering near the ground, a feeling I get on the lower deck.

I love the museum where I work. We own some of the finest art and artefacts in the world, and what's on show is only the tip of the iceberg. But for space we could treble or quadruple our exhibits. Yet what is missing in our vast collection interests me more than what is there. I am sure that has to do with my being a refugee. Because we have been deracinated, we are condemned to yearn. Imagine you stand accused of theft, you have not committed the crime and you are stunned into silence, and before you can protest your hand is cut off. Your severed hand lies on the block and all that is left is the twitch in your arm, and a craving for that phantom hand. That is what they did with our history, and we are left twitching at times, my brother and I, and when it gets too bad we call for help. That is all we do, call for help. That's not unreasonable.

As for women, Fabrice is the keen one, and at times when I have followed his devouring pursuits I have felt twinges of apprehension about my own sexuality. I have watched him eye girls, and their response makes him sit up, and some cooing inside him breaks at his lips to make him smile, and before long they sit together and begin some amorous intrigue. I am too shy for that. It takes me time to get used to someone, let alone to undress in front of them. I have had only two short affairs in the past fifteen years, and I blame Fabrice for my celibate existence. He occupies that space where others put up their lovers, and that is why I can't have anyone stay in my life. Their hovering, when I tried to live with someone, disturbed my privacy too much. Besides, I was never sure for how long my feelings would let me feel what I wanted to feel, and in the end I could no longer live with that frightening prospect, to be left with a complete stranger in my flat. At times though, I must admit, I do have a glow-worm affair, one single bright night. That's when the weed of sex drives through my concrete no matter how hard I try to keep it out.

Fabrice has always liked insects, and I remember when we played as children that he allowed ants to crawl on his hand, and the way he picked up wasps when they landed on his plate when we ate on the veranda in Jo'burg. I detest them, as did my mother. She often walked about with a fly-whisk which she knew how to wield with ruthless accuracy. I think of this now as I realize I am hovering exactly like a bee before it lands on coloured petals to suck nectar. Fabrice is the problem. To describe him I have to be careful not to offend either of us. There is, however, a simple way to solve my dilemma. Let him speak. That way, should he offend, I shall be the victim, and I can take that more easily than to give him offence, or to offend myself. I have his diaries and journals, and I shall use these as instructed by him. Let me tell you how I obtained those books of his.

Three years ago, after a decade of restless existence when he lived in various parts of Europe, Fabrice came back to England to settle, and I found him a room in Frau Eppstein's house round the corner. He had kept in touch by writing occasional letters, and by sending at least his address to Maman so that she would know where to remit her monthly allowance to him. When he arrived the first thing that struck me was that his uncanny sense of timing was still unimpaired, for he arrived at my door within a minute or so of my coming home from the museum. His face looked taut, his skin spanned tighter than mine, but on closer inspection I decided that it was simply the hot sun over Greece that had disturbed our likeness. That's where he had lived the last year, in Monemvassia, at the foot of the Peloponnese.

'Nobody knows', he told me soon after he had arrived, 'that I'm a great poet. If only', he laughed, 'I could get it down on paper!'

Unlike me Fabrice has an infectious laugh. You hear him laugh and laugh as well, though he stops as abruptly as he begins. He cannot sustain anything for long.

'Read this,' he said, handing me a folded sheet of paper he had pulled from his shirt pocket. 'It's the beginning of something great, I tell you, man.'

He has kept his South African accent, whereas over the years I have lost mine. There were three lines on that sheet, in writing I could hardly decipher. He did not care about my lack of comment when I handed it back to him, and I believe he had carried about that beginning of something for some time, simply as a talisman he could attribute to his power. That first evening we talked into the night and between reminiscences we filled the gaps which had appeared between us through living apart for so long. We talked about Maman and her weakness for umbrellas. Fabrice, years ago, had started to call her Madame Parapluie, and it was amusing once more to hear him call her that. 'She wants us to have style, Madame Parapluie.' He laughed when he said that, and complained that his monthly allowance from home was not enough for him to live in style. 'She sends me just enough to keep going and squanders her dough on brollies.'

I happen to know how much he got from her each month, for over the years she boasted about the amounts she sent him, which were not too generous. Her reasons, which she explained in detail when she visited London, which she did every eight months, were quite sound. Beyond a certain minimum, she maintained, he would squander every penny and go in for more drugs than he was already taking. That's what my money would go on, instead of better food and better living.

Five months ago, an hour before he was once more taken

12

away, Fabrice gave me his diaries and journals. He had done so before when he had gone off for treatment, to hold them for safe keeping, and I never dipped into them. They comprised, he said, his real work. The rest he was prepared to scrap and start again, or destroy, as he had done with so much of his work. It included, I know, some superb poems, and much unfinished work with marvellous beginnings. He told me once he had called his bathtub the Ganges, and lying there like Poseidon he had set light to screwed-up pages of his manuscripts, thinking that the soul of what he had written would enter his godhead that way.

His room in Frau Eppstein's house faces the garden at the back, a scruffy bit of lawn with trees too high to allow things to grow. Frau Eppstein doesn't care about her garden and has allowed the trees to take over. Some weeds grow near the brick walls, but even they aren't vigorous and straddle the caked soil, which hasn't been worked for years. Fabrice was calm as we waited, incapable, it seemed, of uttering another word. That's why I stared out of the window, not knowing what else to do. From my own hands I could see that Fabrice was trembling as I felt the current of terror course through our veins. As he waited for the knock at the door the thugs had him trapped, the animal was netted and waiting to be transported to the zoo. If only his room had been to the front of the house I could have laid bets with myself that the fifth or the eighth vehicle would be the ambulance, and we could have gone down to meet the two nurses as they arrived at the front door.

When the bell rang Fabrice said, 'Here they come, the two ponces in clone gear!' He pretended to look nonchalant. 'I'll receive them in the library. Frau Eppstein will let them in and everything inside her knickers will go tight. Once a refugee, always a refugee,' he quipped. 'It'll remind her of Berlin in '38, the Gestapo coming for her husband.'

I picked up his books when they knocked at the door. Fabrice had suddenly become lively and amused. One of the male nurses offered to carry the haversack into which he had stuffed his sponge-bag and pyjamas.

'I travel light,' he said, laughing at them. Then he turned to me. 'And this time,' he commanded me as I followed him downstairs, 'read the stuff, use it, water your garden with it. You've got my permission, man, I'll sign a document, a Deed of Assignment, the bin is full of lawyers, I bet. I'll have it drawn up and sent to you by special messenger, or by telex.'

Frau Eppstein was standing by the front door with her hand outstretched, but Fabrice forgot to shake it, so she let it drop. As he mounted the ambulance he called out to me, 'Eat plenty of iron. It's good for you. Piano-strings are best. Chew them!'

I don't go on nostalgia trips with Fabrice, because it is not befitting. I don't yearn for stars on cloudy nights because I know they are there lighting up the sky above the clouds. They are a remote presence in the firmament from which poets suck ideas. Fabrice has that star quality. When the ambulance drove off I felt stunned by his abrupt departure and then I decided this time to read his journals and diaries which I was holding in my arms as if they were his head. Then I laughed as I recalled one of my visits to Paris when Fabrice was living in that attic in the Cit de Coeur. As I walked in he was on the phone, the earpiece was a ball of wool, blue, I remember, and the lead extended right across the room and was connected to the skein necklaced about the back of a chair. He laughed when he saw me and put the phone down. Next day, without knowing where I was going, he met me at the foot of the escalator at the Galeries Lafayette. A day later I was having lunch at a restaurant when in he walked and sat down at my table as if all this had been arranged beforehand. Fabrice knows how to converge. He stays in touch. That's why I laughed. He wasn't far away and could appear at any moment and stand next to me.

Two

Dürer would have been no good at painting Fabrice's hands.
Soutine, yes. A splash of vermilion would show the twist of his
thumbs curving outwards which make his fingers look stiff, as
if he'd never use them. Unlike mine, his hands tremble a good
deal. His handwriting is large and irregular, a seismograph of
the tremors inside him. Much of his writing I cannot decipher
easily, and I doubt whether he can after some time has passed.
Many of his pages have doodles at the sides, and there are whole
sheets of them which remind me of Art Brut, but at a second
glance I find a capricious streak which spoils purity, and
doodles they remain. But that's not important.

This time I decided to read his journals from cover to cover,
and when I had done so I felt enriched to the point of wishing to
share his 'work' with others. That's when the idea of
transcribing Fabrice's journals came to me. I spent several days
resisting the urge to go ahead, but in the end succumbed. In the
first place, I suppose, my need for tidiness and order drove me
to my task. Above all, though, arid tracts of my own life were
suddenly watered by my twin's adventures, he led me to
gardens of the mind I had never visited before and I became
enthralled by his guidance. When he is well again I'll show him
what I have done.

So it starts - Book One, he calls it.

*   *   *

15

This is Book One but not necessarily the beginning.

I sit tied to a chair and my mother gives instructions to our maid to beat my thighs with a black umbrella. The maid herself is black and follows her mistress's instructions to the letter. Louise has been carefully tutored by Madame Parapluie in torturing anything from chickens to men. There is a large picture of Irma Greese in my mother's bedroom right above her bed, a place reserved in the houses of the devout for effigies which, if you come to think of it, are no less cruel. Louise applies the rod to perfection. If it weren't for the pain she inflicts, the way she swings her hips, the umbrella an extension of her strong, supple arm, would be a sight to delight in. At impact her hip becomes as if she had a folded vertebra inside her back which unfolds at certain moments to give her extra height, as when she swings her arse as she walks or dances to the drums the boys beat for her at dusk. Trust that black bitch to have learnt her craft well under the tutelage of that white cow! Scratch a Negro and you'll find a slave. It is high time, though, we offered ourselves as victims.

It is early morning. They've let the chickens out of their coops but not yet fed them their grain. Nor have the dogs in the neighbourhood been fed. My screams are drowned by their infectious barking and the hideous sound of chickens, as if some ghostly surgeon were stalking the yard stabbing their vocal chords. The feathers plucked off Tuesday's bird still lie ungathered. The blacks are superstitious about feathers; they'll burn them in the next fire they'll make. To touch them may bring back the animal they've killed in a shape as vicious as their killing. They're shit-scared of that.

I've just killed a wasp that's come in through the balcony door. I am living at the top of Frau Eppstein's house, where I occupy two rooms. A lot of insects come flying in and as a rule I leave them alone or help them to the open window so they can fly away. I took several swipes at that wasp to kill it and thought: could that creature be a striped Samson which could rally its strength once more and attack me? I scooped it up and threw it over the balcony railing into the garden. Its last flight,

I promise you.

Meet my analyst. Nine months ago I gave him the boot. He was a nice enough fellow, my Ernst. Not once during our thrice-weekly sessions did he fall asleep. Quite a feat, that, as every ten minutes or so of brash outpourings and tangential asides, whatever went on in that Jungian sieve came out as common as amen, the preacher's versicle being the only form of conversation between us, our soul contact, an unchanging litany leaving me exactly as before, unchanged. Everything, he told me, goes back to the first three or four weeks (or is it months?) of your life. Let me go back to your mother's engagement ring – a sapphire, you said. Correct? You mentioned that with so much emphasis when you told me about the Nazi official who pulled it off her finger when you handed in your jewellery in '38 whilst Papa was in hiding. Was it after the Night of the Long Knives? No, the *Krystallnacht*, I correct him. Ah, yes, of course. He wanted to pick his nose at this point but only scratched it and adjusted the bridge of his glasses. They kept sliding down. There, I was right. He let his finger come down his nose, tilted his head back and let it rest above his top lip. There we go, one or two prods up his nostril, first one, then the other, the other a compensatory action for the one he'd picked first. But, to be fair, he didn't go up high and kept his finger clean. He's on about some profundity. That fear you have of Annie – she's French, that's the one? *Oui*. Crossing the road is, of course, your own fear being projected on to your friend. This fear starts very early. It is possible, more than likely, that your mother's ring, say, scratched your arm. I'll find, I tease fishface, some tiny scar on my arm to prove his point. He smiles. Or its metal, as she held you, pressed too hard against your tender rib-cage and hurt you. In short, her fear of dropping you expressed by her tight hold entered you. What conjecture! I don't think my mother ever held me tight. You were always a terror, my dear. You sucked so hard my nipples were sore after a week. I'm sure I preferred, I tell fishhead, the smooth teat when I took to the bottle they'd bought at Stiefel's the chemist. Was Frau Stiefel the first woman to bewitch me? There's no reason why she

17

should have been different before I can remember her. She used to give us a sweet whenever we went there with our nurse, and dipped her manicured hand into a glass jar, where she groped until she got hold of the bonbon. I watched her and observed her nail polish which left her cuticles uncovered, half-moons to disturb my nights. E. doesn't know what to make of that. Ah, yes, he says, we must go back to that next time. We never do. I can't take E.'s fishing for the truth seriously. We never caught a single fish, and I've become as indifferent to shrinks as Mengele was to his child patients. Not, God forbid, that I am in any way like the famous Auschwitz doctor. See for yourself, He's coming for lunch.

It's twenty-eight degrees, it'll be over thirty by noon and I want to go to the pool. There's nowhere in the house one can be comfortable. But my mother won't let me. Not until after lunch. Uncle Jo is coming. As soon as we've finished eating you can be off. As a rule you can't rely on what she says, but today she means it. At siesta time she'll want us out of the way. And today would be dangerous to disobey her as she's geared up to play Frau Friedrich Edel von Breitenbach, that's one of Mengele's assumed names under which he travels from his Paraguayan hide-out to his loved ones in Günzburg, Austria. She's wearing – I saw her at eleven and she's ready for Jo, and she won't move much before he arrives so as not to crease her clothes – a khaki skirt smooth as marble and a Sam Browne across her bulge. She carries a khaki umbrella. She's put a splash of carmine on her lips and removed her nail polish. Louise answers the door. I watch from the landing. My mother is more excited than I've seen her in years and greets Uncle Jo with open arms. Clumsy cow. She drops her brolly at the moment of climax. Perhaps she was frightened he might have mistaken her raised arm for the old salute. He looks cool. Once a natty dresser, always a natty dresser. At Auschwitz he always wore sharply creased uniforms, polished boots, and white gloves. His trousers are neat, his shoes shine and – my God! – even in this heat he wears gloves, which he removes, that defrocked surgeon, with a dexterity acquired in former times.

I'd forgotten he had a squint. As I come into the sitting-room just before lunch he turns to me, his legs and what have you stiffen as he remains seated, and smiles so I can see that famous triangular cleft on his upper front teeth. 'He's grown, little Fab,' he comments, not addressing the prisoner but the wardress in charge. I scan his pockets for a tubular bulge to see whether he's carrying a syringe. His looks pendulate between me and that stupid cow. 'But still a child,' he adds, in full smile.

He'd like to do something to me, I can feel it, pinch my cheeks, insert his finger into my mouth and make me say *aah* till I choke. He keeps holding his smile like a breath. After injecting benzine into his unsuspecting victims, that's how he dispatched them to their death, smiling.

Tuesday's chicken stinks. At best there's not much meat on them but what there is on that miserable carcass is high. Jo, being used to stenches worse than that, doesn't notice. Nor does Irma. She's interested only in picking up her own scent. Every few minutes, it's one of her endearing habits, she bends her head down, her nostrils veer towards her cleavage where she's put on scent and, if her sniff is disappointing, out comes her spray and she starts squirting. They'd eat shit, those two, provided it was served on clean plates. I don't have to wait for coffee, so as soon as I've had a fig for dessert I'm off to the pool. Am I glad to get away! Mengele stared at me as I left, and as I ran out of the house and down the road I felt his stare stick to me like a burr.

I should have gone to the police to report matters. I'd just turned thirteen and that year I'd started to have sleepless nights, for which the doc had prescribed some white pills. Four at a time did the trick. They made me sleep all right, but then for two days I used to walk about unsteady like a pissed dog. The police would have snapped at me, would have called my mother, who'd have come down at once to haul me away. Between them, who knows, they might even have put me inside. Or she'd have had me beaten like a black, got Louise on the job with an array of umbrellas every day for a week to teach me a lesson. Perhaps I should have tried the Jewish authorities, the Board of

19

Guardians. But why come to us, they'd have asked, why not go to the police? Who are you? Fabrice Korn. Jewish? Yeah. Where were you barmitzwa'd, which *schule*? I wasn't. What I can tell them? My father, a Viennese jeweller, was murdered on the beach by one of my mother's lovers. By all accounts he was a lousy shit, though all accounts come from her, Irmgard, my mother, that cow. No one else knew him - no one, that is, except a few whores and some louts who fleeced him at poker. In the end I had to take his money away from him, else we'd have been destitute, my mother keeps telling us to this day whenever she talks about him. And she's hung on to it ever since, his money and his precious stones. Now and again she raids her Aladdin's cave and sells a diamond or two to top up her funds and buys a few more umbrellas. The rest she keeps for a rainy day.

I might as well get rid of our father, which shouldn't take long because I know little about him. That twin and I were five when we arrived in Jo'burg in '38, via Naples. My mother says her corset was pinching all the way from Vienna and some of the precious stones round her middle made her bleed. There aren't any photographs of my father anywhere, we have to rely on Maman's description of him, which doesn't satisfy me one bit. Tall he was, with a broad chest. My mother says he would have grown fat with age because of his passion for *Sachertorte*. She keeps denigrating him even for being in a state he never reached. For the size of her face she's got a big mouth.

Miranda the gypsy read my palm when Louise took me to the Witwatersrand Fair. My mother had told us about the gypsies in Vienna, how people locked their doors when they came to beg and to sell clothes-pegs. They could give you the evil eye and curse you with whatever wicked thought came into their head. The gypsy held my hand very tight and brought it close to her face every time she prepared my palm for a read by crossing it with her thumb to smoothe the flesh. She didn't speak and then looked at Louise who was standing over me, and started to cry. I thought it was part of her act, some trick she performed, as if to make out she was seeing something so terrible or wonderful

20

that she'd ask for more money before she told you what it was. Several times she looked at my eyes. I was frightened at first to look at hers, then summoned what courage I had and caught her stare, black granite spilling with tears. And the sounds she made, wailing whenever she went back to my hand, as if the Devil were dancing on my palm. Poor orphan, she said to Louise, the father's dead and the mother's a witch. There's chaos for the child. Then she got up and put her hand in the pocket of her embroidered apron and gave Louise back the money she'd collected on our way into her booth. Crazy woman, Louise called her. She bought me a stick of candyfloss as big as my head, which I licked to size so I could see where I was going.

I can't ever remember my mother without a man, though none have left a lasting impression. They were in and out of the house like insects. Sometimes even after they'd gone they were there still, lurking on the wall or behind some books or on the floor camouflaged by the pattern of the carpet. You kept on hearing their buzz, and fear stayed switched on whilst you waited for their sting, and you didn't touch the food in case it had gone rotten with their shit. What a disgusting bitch! She always made me feel I was in the way and she chiselled me with her wilfulness to make an image of me which had to contend with my reality and the discontent of her creative ability, poor cow. She cheats all the time and doesn't make me feel safe. I wish she'd hide her clothes from me, we should never have lived under the same roof. I see her pants in the wash-house, her corsets, her stockings a wet ball one moment and ten minutes later blown dry in the sun waiting for the insertion of her legs. Maybe they're for me, her clothes. They're going to cut off my prick and dress me in her clothes. My pants on the line reassure me but don't take away the haunting of her evil intent.

All the time we grew taller. My brother and I marked the cupboard with our height and grew towards safety. I made plans for when I was even with her, delightful musings. I knew pretty well what she found abominable and set my course to scare the daylights out of her. There'd come a time when I could take swipes at her like she did for sport when going after insects with her fly-whisk. She killed with relish and then was too squeamish to peel the dead flies off the cushions and window-panes.

Jo Mengele and Muttchen knew each other in the old days. They went hiking together in the Austrian Alps and attended yodelling competitions. Though I find it hard when I look at most people to believe they've fucked in their lives, I believe without a shadow of doubt that my mother has fucked every man she's ever talked to for more than three minutes. You can tell from the way she holds her umbrella. She never has a firm hold on the handle but rubs it with her fingers to make one believe she can unbend the curve in her hot palm. She spends hours at her dressing-table, not only first thing in the morning but often during the day, studying her effect on men, as if she knew how to write messages on her face with her eyebrow pencil and rouge whilst quietly yodelling to herself. Having had her to ourselves for years I've had time to study her, at least from the outside. The rest I imagine. She makes me. Oh yes, don't think she's some innocent cow left a young widow with a right to sympathy! When there aren't men around fingering their way to her coiled approach she has female friends who inveigle me into their world with outrageous words and gestures and a complete lack of respect for my sex. Every time one of them comes she inspects me to see whether I'm ready for the oven, like the witch who prodded Hänsel in his cage. Or whether perhaps the time has come for me to wear high heels. If that's not what they're thinking, why do they keep on talking about nothing but clothes and fashion, the latest import of silk underwear from Italy and new perfumes from France? With Mengele my mother's powerful friend, what friend have I? My twin brother? Who knows what he really thinks inside his skin. Who will help me fight these women when they come, to take me away to abuse me, for their way is the way of the world and my life is in their hands, and I am merely their feeble victim, the fly caught in their conspiratorial web.

22

Here, for several pages, Fabrice's writing goes off the page, over the edge, and I can't make out a single word. What is strange, though, and what gives these pages some kind of visual form, is the fact that every line ends in a stroke right to the end of the line, as if beyond that the writing would once more become legible. I don't know whether Fabrice ever showed E. what he had written, and what E. would have made of it. Rain on his brain, cloudbursts, the ferrules of dozens of mother's umbrellas, that's my interpretation, for a few pages later there are doodles of brollies half-opened, winging their way like vicious birds with hooked beaks sharp as sickles. Next, their cloth is taut and depicted from above – two whole pages are covered like that. They look as if they were on the move, the slightest touch sets them in motion and you look for the one which moved first, but the creatures fool you and are still as woodlice disturbed during their tedious crawl. Then follows a page of finely drawn, arched canopies of umbrellas joined to form a spider's web. At the centre the spider sits, drawn in red ink. Next page Fabrice goes on. I have put three on top.

A pause, though, before we go on, to allow me to state that, after careful consideration, I've decided not to pass comment on Fabrice's journals as I transcribe them, however much I am tempted to do so at times. I admit this was not a difficult decision to make. From my work at the museum I am used to respecting the work of others, and exhibiting it. And my temperament, which makes me inclined to stand back, also stands me in good stead to fulfil my task without interfering.

Three

Paris, France. Meet Annie, Mademoiselle Purcelle. She's not averse to dope and we smoke it most evenings, not the good Afghan stuff we're sometimes given by our friend downstairs, but cheap Moroccan kef which is good enough to enlarge our attic to palatial size. Today Annie's hands are grubby and her tousled hair's in need of a wash. It's lost its sheen. She says we're in a state together, there's a skin engulfing us - can't you see? she asks when the dope hits her gills - and we mustn't damage it with soap and water. I like the way she peels her clothes off, then mine, and then drives me frantic with licked hands and draws me to her to let me spend everything I've got inside her. Purcellina, my crumpet voluntary. I call her that when I start teasing her to give me the best dope there is. Her dad is a *capitaine* in the French army. Annie says he has an irritating twitch when he moves his left arm. The right one came off when he stood too near the fireworks when they scuttled the fleet at Toulon. We avoid the Trocadéro, where her parents have a posh apartment opposite the Eiffel Tower, for Annie is supposed to be in London learning English.

I met her in London. Summer surprised us, coming over Russell Square with a shower of rain. I'd stopped in the colonnade to watch the Berlitz girls stream out at four and spotted bright-lipped Annie as she opened her parapluie. She walked off to the right, but when the wind drove the rain against her neat clothes, she turned back and came to shelter

24

next to me. We went for a coffee and talked for an hour and laughed at language, at appalling English and French. We lied, saying we could read it better than speak it. She came back to my place and stayed for two days. Then she had to go, as the cow was coming to graze in Earls Court. Also, after two days, she needed fresh clothes. Not that later on she would have stood in such need. It's amazing how quickly Annie's Parisian chic became lost, how she adapted herself to my filthy sheets which Frau Eppstein at times, out of the goodness of her heart, changed because I hadn't bothered to go to the laundry for six weeks. Her torn stockings weren't replaced, her make-up, though she still painted her lips every day, became caked and split from disuse like Marilyn Monroe's toiletries which were sold at auction a year after her supposed suicide. I liked that little detail when I read about it in the papers. And then there was Lantelme, a Parisian beauty who died in mysterious circumstances travelling up the Rhine in her husband's yacht. At the sale of her fabulous clothes her underwear was passed from hand to hand along the row of buyers before they made their bids. I liked that too. I like women's stuff, their clothes, those garments not made for men. I feel them being worn, but not on myself, feet raised on heels on which I sometimes pretend to walk. I raise myself on my toes to see what effect this has on the small of my back and the area of the groin. To balance myself I push out my chest, and love Annie with her bosom extended, carrying her sex in a way I can't share with her. So many things, though, I can share with her and get my fair share of understanding, but that which is Annie is locked out, and sometimes I lust for that forbidden fruit. I'd like to be her for a bit. I talked about my yearning to E., it's of old standing and was particularly strong with Marie-Claire after she left Picasso. Of that later, when no one's around. I described for E. some of the women who constantly visited my mother when I was a child, *en masse* a terror to my senses in that cathouse, but individually, as I recorded them with uncanny accuracy, sweet and amusing, but none the less aggressive in their smart clothes with their made-up faces. One or two of them have since died in action, others are on the retired list, some still wear their decorations, whenever the occasion allows, particularly Frau Horngrad, stiff round the middle as her name implies, the Litvak *corsetière* who seduced the husband of one of her clients in front of eight witnesses whilst his wife was being fitted in the next cubicle of her Jo'burg salon. Having made sure of eight witnesses for her heroic deed, she got the VC for that. E. had nothing to say on the subject, the arsehole. I wasted my time trying to amuse him, and E. mine. Whenever a fish came near the hook he immediately withdrew the rod and cast once more, going back to the beginning, the first three weeks of my life, or three months. What an arsehole!

Had a long talk with Frau Eppstein this morning. She likes Annie and asks why didn't I introduce her to *La Dama de Peraguas* when she visited London. Nobody believes me when I tell them she bought five new umbrellas in two days whilst she was here. It obviously fulfils some phallic need. Next time, I tell Frau Eppstein, I'll introduce her. Whilst patting the pillows she's just changed she shakes her head in disbelief. There won't be a next time. She doesn't say that, but a feeling of cramp in my stomach murmurs what her thinking predicts. Such a nice girl, but as *schlampig* as you are. Look at her clothes on the floor. She picks up Annie's discarded clothes and carefully hangs them in the wardrobe next to my pants and jackets. A shame such nice things to treat like that. It's five months we've stayed in London, and, have I told you, Frau Eppstein, we're going away next week for a month or two? To Paris, France. How nice. To see Marie-Claire and Chaim. I haven't seen Soutine for over a year. How nice. She's hanging up Annie's red skirt with the pleats – boy, I feel like putting my hand inside, just seeing it swing as Frau Eppstein reaches for the rod inside the wardrobe. When she's gone I'll put Annie's clothes back on the floor. Got to be careful not to touch Annie's butterfly feelings or I'll have her dust on my fingers and she'll die. Don't touch, don't come too close, dear, don't stifle me, not too much sharing, keep away. There are warning signs all over her: *S curve, road narrows, T junction!* But cat's-eyes light my route to her at night, we leave the curtains undrawn and the light from the street or the sky, whichever is stronger, is sufficient for me to see that marvellous landscape which vies with beauty with what I dream about.

Curse my dreams. Her nearness is a wall beyond which I ford the river to reach Canaan, the Promised Land. I've scaled that wall many times, using bits and pieces of rope floating about my head to make a ladder. The other day someone told me about false photographs, a picture you see of a model in glossy magazines, he said, isn't all that same person. Her beautiful head, the chin resting on an outstretched hand with long fingers, the head belongs to one, the hand to someone else. A composite beauty made up of different girls, where does one begin, another end? What is it with me when I lie with Annie that I think of Monroe, or Mr Thompson's wife with her narrow waist and pursed lips, of Rosa's legs, her thighs in particular, and of those untouchable females, around when I was a child, who have left me with fear intact and who punish me, those innocents, so that I can mask my inadequacy? How long can I go on and find food for my feeble sex?

Be calm, darling, Annie tells me, there. She goads me and removes one obstacle after another with her strokes and kisses, keeps on undressing me long after I've no clothes left on. Nor does she frighten away those ghosts in my head which I will need when I'm alone once more, when she goes to sleep, when I'll watch over her for a time and with gossamer thoughts try to worm myself into her brain to share her dreaming. It's all right for a time – not for long, though, I can't keep it up, can't keep connecting. I lose control and don't know what to do other than lose myself. Another joint, or, if it's the time of the month when my allowance has come, a few more sniffs, or three or four tablets. I've got to calm down, get back to normal after I've been wild with Annie, bitten and licked her, played rumbustuous games with her, like a dog gone wild for meat, and she teasing and yielding – God, the noise we make I'm sure Frau Eppstein thinks it's Henze we sometimes play as loud as it'll go with the door open to soften suspicion when our climax comes.

I don't like it when I start itching all over. It can start at any time, whether I'm hot or cold, and I've had allergy tests done by some Harley Street ponce who asked me the most absurd questions. He read from a questionnaire, which was for both men and women, and left it to me to give him the picture. Do you put cream on your face, wear make-up? (What make?) What clothes do you wear next to your skin? He went through every garment you can think of, ticking his list, and I was tempted to say yes to girdle and tights to see whether he'd lift his head to take a look at me, the arsehole. He was dead serious and didn't approve of my giggles which interrupted the flow of his monotone. Afterwards he made various smears on my arm, all in different colours which he then blotted on to glass slides for examination under a microscope. He gave me some pills to get on with and made an appointment for a week ahead. I ate the pills on the bus on my way home. They did nothing for me and I didn't keep the next appointment with that stupid fart. There's buzzing in my head, I can switch it on and listen to it at any time but often don't bother for days. The slightest cold makes me a bit deaf and then the noise in my head gets worse because I can't hear much else. I laugh louder when I've got a cold, and use my long-distance voice, but I don't suppose anyone notices.

We were in Paris for Annie's birthday. She left me for a couple of days to go home to her parents and then came back all cleaned up in her Parisian chic. I don't suppose Sabatine, the concierge, told Annie to introduce me to her parents. Some difference between her and Frau Eppstein. Sabatine's husband is a sewer rat who comes scraping at our door the first day of each month to collect the rent. If you don't happen to be in funds that day he screams at you in his gutter language, calls you a stinking drug-pusher or worse, and threatens you with *la police* if your money's not there by six that night. Twice he's called the gendarme when my money hasn't arrived through some quirk at the bank. Now when he comes to collect I give him a glass of wine, and the moment it touches his lips he eulogizes over the bottle, says it's much better than that gut-rot Sabatine provides. The room is cheap enough, a hundred francs a month, so we don't vacate it even when we go back to England or to foreign parts.

Three years ago I decided I needed England for its language and hospitals and for the protection my brother could afford to give me. Whilst in France I'd been taken to a nut-house in Clichy, and I swear to you that the nurses carry batons which they use freely at certain times of the day. They come in unshaven at six in the morning, male and female nurses, and call out *bonjour à Beaujon* whilst they walk down the wards and rattle their batons against the iron bedsteads. Beaujon is a cold place, there aren't enough blankets, so you scatter what clothes you have on top of you for extra warmth and by the time you wake up you're just about warm enough to feel faintly comfortable. Then those evil drones start you off on another day of torture. It's best when you are really sick, when there's ringing in your head so loud it threatens to break your skull and you lie there like a crashed mountaineer, listless in pain, and cold and heat are all the same. Imagine them coming at you in that state, using their batons to uncover you and chase you out of bed, and then they stand over you and watch you douse your face in cold water and brush your teeth. Believe me, England is gentler to its sick. Even Calaban who looked after us in the strong-room at Shenfield was an angel compared with Fabian at Beaujon. Ask Shostakovich. It so happens he was with me in both places. At Shenfield he tuned the piano all day long.

I don't like being left out in the cold, Annie spending her birthday with her mother and that one-armed bandit of a father. For once I wanted Maman to be at hand to give a dinner party at Maxim's, to which she could have invited *le capitaine* and his escort. I'd have made sure they'd served one of those tough charollais steaks the Frogs are so fond of, just to watch the sweat of embarrassment break out on his pale brow until someone offered to saw his meat into small bits for him. That cow is never to hand when she's wanted. Most likely she's lechering about the Cape with Martin Bormann. I've heard

29

rumours that he's had a number tattooed on his arm and performs as a Jewish yodeller in Jo'burg night-clubs. So I had to take matters into my own hands and arrange some celebration for Annie's birthday. That was just prior to my sojourn at Clichy.

This is what we did.

I don't know whether our feast was inspired by Rembrandt or Soutine – the latter, I should imagine. Apart from Soutine and Marie-Claire, neither of whom could attend, I asked half a dozen of our friends to meet us at the Restaurant des Artistes to celebrate. That afternoon I went to the Rue de Vaugirard and paid a visit to the slaughterhouse, where I purchased the carcass of a pig. I wondered whether Sabatine thought I'd committed child murder when I brought that large parcel through the door. I'd had it wrapped up in brown paper, but it was cumbersome to carry, and the best way I found was to hold it in my arms like a child. I didn't want to take it all the way upstairs and left it by the side of the cupboard on the first landing. Not wishing to let Sabatine know what I was doing – she went crazy if someone left anything on the landing – I waited for as long as it would take me to get to our room and back again before going out to buy a bottle of sparkling wine to send us on our way for a good evening. On my return Annie was starkers in bed waiting for me. Her eyes were nicely glazed and as I bent down to kiss her I remarked that the rich food she'd been eating at home had gone straight to her eyes. Don't, she said, don't make joke today. The sweet smell of a joint hung in the air and mixed where she lay with the Joy I'd bought her for a present. She tugged at my trousers, played with my belt to loosen it, then turned away, her head only, playing a form of hide-and-seek. Next when I look at you there will be your beautiful head in any arms. I think she'd been playing with herself, she was wet as oil and started to miaow the moment I touched her. Sometimes she was like that, ravenous, completely obsessed with her need to have me come inside her big and fast, lynching and being lynched at the same time, that tiny nigger inside her trapped in her burning barn until it emerged bright as

30

phosphorus and then, like a glow-worm, went out like a light.

We slept for an hour and then I told her a dream I'd just had. We stood under the waterfall at En Gedi and made love, with the water falling over us, in sight of the Dead Sea, exactly the spot where David had his bath after slaying Goliath. I know, she said, and embraced me. She said we'd keep our clothes on, and by the time we'd walked a few yards they were dry. That marvellous heat, she said. We dreamed together. I was there too. I don't trust Annie, the little devil. Don't let's go out, she said, I want you again. She wouldn't let me get out of bed and we lay in each other's arms for another ten minutes or so. Then she got up and asked me to open the bottle while she went for a pee.

I'm not in charge. I keep chasing her. Something is wrong. We've got to go out soon to meet the others. There's no time to sort things out before we go. There never is. When there is time I don't know what is wrong. When she came back to the room she dressed without saying a word. If you are living in one room you can't hide, and you notice everything. Clouds travel across the ceiling. One moment it's light, the next it's dark. Perhaps putting her clothes on she felt shy about having allowed me to see her naked.

The bubbly put Annie into a good mood. And me. On our way down I picked up the parcel, and although she was curious to know what was inside, Annie assumed it was another present for her and didn't push her curiosity too far, *la petite bourgeoise*. When we got to the restaurant the others were waiting at our table, their presents for Annie neatly wrapped in front of them, which they handed to her as she did her round of greetings. That gave me time to put the pig on a chair, where I unwrapped it and made it sit up as if it were one of our party. There were shrieks when they all saw it, of laughter as well as disgust. Solange, sitting next to it, made the most noise and almost fell off her chair. Annie laughed and laughed. I knew she would. It was, to be sure, a hilarious sight, this gutted carcass with its head on and two of its hoofs on the table to keep it sitting upright. The waiter came up to me and told me in a most

31

unfriendly tone that I couldn't behave like this in a French restaurant. Behave like what, man? I asked him. Bring in a pig. But I love her. She's my fiancée. He was disarmed. The moment you mention love in France you win their hearts. '*Je m'excuse, Monsieur,*' he said, and with his pencil poised over his order pad, he asked, 'What will your fiancée have to start with?'

Half-way through the meal, it had started so well, I felt something go wrong. Like a bone cracking in the brain, nothing big, just a tiny bone thin as fuse-wire. It went snap and the light went dim. I suddenly couldn't hear what anyone was saying, colours faded, before long I'd be dead as that pig I'd brought to the table. I don't know. You can't trust what they tell you when you're well again. I remember nothing except waking up in the bin three days later, feeling sore all over as if I'd been at the wrong end of a baton charge. Most likely I had been. I felt bruised and there were patches, I swear, red turned to blue, all over me. I wanted the evidence to be recorded and asked for a photographer, but they wouldn't comply with my request. When you're better, they said, we'll take some snaps, not now. You look terrible. Why take pictures when you look terrible? Madame Philipponat, the doctor in charge, looked severe. Every day about five she came riding into the ward with a posse of male nurses behind her. They wisecracked among themselves, and before leaving she gave instructions on how to feed and water the patient. The ward, I noticed, was locked and the windows barred. Where was Annie? Why didn't she come to visit me? Did she know where I was? Did anyone know? The heaps in the beds next to me were men asleep. Later on I was told we were in for a three-week sedation treatment, and that our pâté and caviare were being fed to us intravenously. I'd woken after two days and become immune to their injections and was then removed to a ward on the ground floor, a real madhouse. The noise there, day and night, was indescribable. But why discuss such ugly things? After a week they let me go and Annie came to fetch me home.

Four

At first the taxi driver refused to go down our narrow street, but Annie insisted and made him stop right outside No. 48. I wished she'd have brought my sun-glasses. The light was so bright it made my eyes blink. I'd been in that cave at Clichy and the late summer sun stung like dying bees and made my skin sore. We got back at the time of day when Sabatine left her cage to cook lunch. We talked in whispers. If she heard us she'd come pouncing out to see who it was. My legs stuttered and I took a long time to walk upstairs. I slumped down on a chair and Annie undid my shoes and helped me out of my clothes, then put me to bed. I'll make some tea, she said. By the time the kettle boiled I was alseep.

I woke in a room by Vermeer. The afternoon sun all over Paris was gathered into one shaft of light blazing through our window. Annie sat at the table, using that light to sew in. I watched her pull the yarn, then take aim to make the next stitch. I'd noticed when I'd come in that whilst I was away Annie had cleaned the place up and moved what little furniture there was into new positions. She was taking care of me. Not since Louise had anyone done that. Sweetheart, I said, I am so happy. She put a finger to her mouth. Ssh. You stay in bed, darling, and rest. A little later I'll make supper. Time was spaced. A little later, she'd said, and after that she'd still be there, tonight and tomorrow. I was overcome by calm and comfort in my head. I lay in that half-state of waking, conscious of that borderline thin as a hair when your eyelids are closed, should I or shouldn't I go back to sleep? If I continue like that the half-light sets off the chemistry of dreams. That day, I clearly remember those juvenescent days of my recovery, I had no wish to dream. I, a temporary alien, had returned to the world. Like soldiers home from battle, their murderous weapons no longer do harm, battlegrounds are cleared, the bones are buried and the blood is washed away by a few showers, by the moisture of dew and the bleaching sun. Annie thinks I've gone back to sleep, she keeps quiet for my sake and continues her sewing. I can hear not the needle pierce the cloth, but the faint screech as she draws the cotton. It is barely a noise. I leaf through books Louise used to read to me before I went to sleep, and come across leaves and grasses we pressed between the pages. They're dry and stiff, their colours are faded. I don't like their sepulchral quality, leave them alone. Don't touch them with your clumsy hands, use them simply as needles to point to those early years on the compass of your life.

All day I've had a fever, at night it rose to crisis point. Dr Menges came, he was there first thing that morning and diagnosed flu. He's a good family friend, knew my father well, and came back at night to comfort my mother. It is hard when sickness visits the bereaved. Papa, they told me, has gone on a long journey, he'll not be back for some time, a long time. They played on time, the time he would take to return, invented twists to lengthen his journey, told me of the adventures he'd described in letters that had arrived. I was easy to hoodwink as I couldn't read, and I became used to his absence and asked no further questions. One can learn not to miss the missing. The doctor's hands were cool, his fingers tapping my chest were hard, more like bone than flesh. Camomile tea, he prescribed, as hot as he can take it. He'll sweat and that'll bring his fever down by the morning. Louise stayed with me all night. After two days I was allowed up for an hour but could manage only half that time. I don't think I ever got my strength back. I was never the same as before. Sickness is like war. Peace returns, but meanwhile change has occurred.

Yet in one's memory old feelings lie encrusted like worn carvings. Sometimes the light of circumstances brings them back into relief and we go fathoms deep into the past. I am unique. No one else has such ragged claws scuttling across the bottom of the silent sea. I feel cleansed and protected, ready to start my work. I've been on deserted islands, walked through sylvan landscapes. I've been on the run, that above all. From nowhere the enemy would suddenly appear and I'd start running. I'm the running Jew, for wandering takes too long these days, they've improved their techniques of harassment. If I don't watch out I'll be dead before I pick up my pen.

The sun has gone from our window. It's gone altogether because the window is dark. Annie, I know, is there. For an hour or so she's been sitting in the dark to watch over me.

'Hi,' I said.

'Hullo, my pet. You've slept a long time. I'm going to put the light on and make supper.'

'Yes I've slept,' I lie. Perhaps it's not a lie. I feel as if I'd dreamed but not had a dream. Perhaps it was the drugs they gave me at Beaujon, for never before in my life have I felt no break between consciousness and what I dreamed. But I don't trust it. I think I've been awake all the time. I tried moving my legs. My body ached, every joint was stiff as if I hadn't used them for months. Those injections they gave me have weakened my muscles. Must drink a lot of water to expel the poison, but it's an effort to swallow. I'm so weak that Annie has to feed me. There's nothing I can do but to leave myself in her hands. Before long I'm gone, I'm absent from everything around me.

* * *

Here Fabrice stops. He leaves seven blank pages. They are neatly numbered at the top but there is no other mark on them, and I suspect one of two things. Either he kept them free to continue the description of his recovery, most likely composed when he was still too weak to hold a pen, and then forgot to copy the stuff from his head on to the paper. Or else the dog in Fabrice found new trails to sniff and abandoned his original pursuit. Whatever the explanation, he was, I am sure, aware that he had left something unfinished, as was so often the case with his writing. We used to talk about it. I've not finished, he used to say and laugh, knowing that he had prevented you once more from judging his work. Though he would have wanted your praise, he did not want to take risks. He loves to tease and make you laugh with him to get you on his side. If I'd finished it and got it published, Maman might have stopped sending me money. Or she'd talk about me to her friends. But at the end of his tomfoolery Fabrice would always be serious, if only for a moment. His face then had a slash of sadness, he couldn't help showing his pain, but in an instant his humour would revive and he would start telling you what next he wanted to write. You knew that that had nothing to do with what he was actually going to produce. Somehow those empty pages are very moving. They evoke expectation and promise. Perhaps they were simply a means of leading us to Alban's story. I don't know how he got to that, how it caught his imagination. He made several attempts to start, crossed out four pages of similar beginnings, then wrote: 'What precision there is in our imagination, and what fumbling in reality.' I think it had more to do with his false starts than with what he was going to write. Anyway, here begins this strange story.

* * *

Five years ago I visited Alban's son in Vienna. I'd gone there with my son, then an impressionable ten-year-old, to show him where I'd lived before the war. It was time, I thought, as now and again I felt some severe pain in my head which the doctors treated as migraine, and some stabbing pains in my chest which threatened, literally, to frighten the life out of me, to show my young heir the graves of my grandparents, so that, if in future he felt inquisitive about the past, he'd know about at least some tendrils of his roots. I am not at all concerned with children having anything to do with death, that they should participate in the rituals of bereavement if and when these occur in the family. On the contrary, keep them away if you can, board them out when it happens, don't let them be taught how to wail by the weird goings-on in a house of the dead. I labour this point to dispel the idea that our return journey, if you can call it that, was in any way morbid. It had nothing to do with any impulse of mine to impart to my child the idea of staying put, of not moving away from where he'd started through me, my parents and theirs, of urging him back by some traceable freak of circumstance to the fourteenth century, a charting rare amongst Jews. No, I simply wanted him to see his name on the tombstones, and the dates of death. I repeat, I object to the young being involved with death, putting on their uncomfortable Sunday best, trying to catch a whiff of the corpse they're trailing behind. That has nothing to do with survival. And I wanted him to glow with the feeling of survival.

I'd been on a similar journey before, with my mother in '48 when the four Allied powers were still in occupation. She had tried, on account of a key in her possession, to get there as soon as the war was over, but no visas were issued then. Finally, after taking the first available boat up the coast of Africa, we landed at Genoa, whence we took the train across the Alps to that smutty city on the banks of the Danube. I shan't describe our visit, but will tell about that key. It fitted, so my mother claimed, a safe deposit box somewhere in that forlorn capital, but she had no idea where it was. She made a list of every bank, gave me two hundred schillings a day to amuse myself in the Prater, and whilst I rose high above the city on the *Riesenrad* she scurried like a famished rat from one bank to another. In the afternoon we met in a coffee-house, and every day she cursed my dead father for his untidy ways, for his selfish neglect of his dependants, his senseless cruelty. I can see him laugh at us from his rotten grave, she once said, digging her fork into a slice of *Schwarzwälder Kirschtorte*, her favourite gunge. By the third day she was utterly dejected. She'd tried the silver and diamond vaults, but nothing was forthcoming. One man had taken the key to the back to compare it, so he'd told her, with one of his keys, and then in his smarmy Viennese manner he'd ushered her out of the shop with deep, heartfelt apologies for not having been able to help. I bet, she said, she'd suddenly thought of it, he took an impression of that key. That's what he did, that swine! I thought I could smell soap. She took the key out of her purse and held it to her nose. I wondered whether perhaps my father had really played a joke on her. A good one, I thought. Any old key would have done the trick.

I took my son to show him the house where we'd lived. It is near the centre, near the Stephansdom, an imposing building five storeys high. We'd lived on the fourth floor, below Dr Bender and his loud and effusive wife. She was friendly enough in those days, and before we left in '38 Maman had sold her some bits and pieces, forbidden books we weren't allowed to possess, some cumbersome Biedermeier furniture and several large tureens superfluous to our requirements. When our furniture arrived in Johannesburg all kinds of things were missing, some of my mother's collection of porcelain and china cups, bits of carved ivory and a Klimt drawing – nothing much, but items evidently selected by a thief with taste. Without hesitation my mother had pointed her finger at Frau Bender. She's the thief, that crass bitch! Her husband, an engineer, she'd once told my mother, used to say *Heil Hitler* in bed when he kissed her good-night. A right number, my mother said, that numbskull. The description suited him, not for his lack of brains, but because the skin on his face was taut and forced him, it seemed, to keep his mouth open and show his large teeth. Dangerous, my mother used to warn. And she was right. Without ado or apologies, on days when the order was given to hoist flags, our dining-room was swathed in a dark red hue, the Benders' huge flag with its giant swastika covering our dining-room window and blocking our view to the street. It fluttered in the wind and swished like a whip, and when it was wet the red cloth stuck to our window-panes, the entrails of a monstrous insect simulating death before it unsucked itself to fly off once more. And in the street below the military band leading hordes of Brownshirts through the city. Once or twice I watched them from another room which had a parapet balcony. I was less afraid then of heights than I am now, but suspect that my vertigo started on that narrow ledge.

Dr Bender once saw me catch a glimpse of what was going on below, and when I called on him with my son he said, 'I remember you watching them march. Oh, how you wished you could have joined them, tra tra tra boom, marching through the streets. They did march well - splendid, wasn't it? They weren't all bad.'

Fortunately my son was out of earshot, else I should have had to take Bender to task about such slander. It disturbed me that he should have harboured a memory like that all these years. There's slander in the very thought. How, I wondered, could I get retribution for such a lie?

'Never,' I said. 'That thought never crossed my mind.'

'Come now, we can speak freely, it's a long time ago. There's nothing to hide. I used to joke about it with my wife. Only six months ago we talked about it, just a few weeks before she passed on, poor dear, how you used to march upstairs with one of your mother's umbrellas at your shoulder, playing at being one of them. Who knows what would have become of you if you'd been able to join them. We were proud of von Schirach when he became the head of the Hitler Youth. A great Austrian poet - have you read his work? Frau Bender's favourite. Greater than Goethe, she used to say. I miss her. I'm now all alone.'

What an arsehole of a man. He offered to make us some real Viennese coffee, which I declined, using my son's dislike of coffee as an excuse. We'd done our bit of spying, had seen some of the missing Meissen in the apartment, though I never told Maman. Whyever not? Didn't I want her to go after Bender to get her stuff back? Perhaps I didn't want Bender to repeat to my mother what he accused me of, wishing to join the Hitler Youth. Since most of what I write is invented, why have I invented this? I got out of the place as fast as I could, and my son followed me.

Poor boy. I'll leave him now. I needed him to start me off for

39

my search into the past, but like most things I invent I cannot sustain him for long. I needed someone to relate to my past and, since there was no one, I invented this young boy with dreamy eyes, stalking my shadow to take over at sunset. I play pleasant games in my head. I get so near to reality that I can invent that boy to the point of touching him, though in the end he evades my touch out of shyness. I see him eat and talk with his mouth full, the way he stands and brings the tips of his fingers together, which gives him that special stance I love so much. Go now, darling.

I spent several days after my Bender encounter in the room of my pension. I was a young child when I left Vienna, so how could that death's-head point an accusing finger at me? Remember, though, that nothing is ludicrous if you stand accused. We'd often played with mother's umbrellas in the house, using them as foils and weapons, extending the power of our short arms. The accused has time disturbance, fear can destroy the sequence of events, confessions can be obtained, and they can put you up against the wall and have you shot before you've got time to retract. For days my mind was in a state of ferment, raced like a clock gone berserk, keeping time but not true time, the Viennese waltz I called it to the empty walls, twisting me round and round with smooth and even steps, gyrating me to dizziness. Maman is a stickler for draughts, and for days I'd not opened my window in order to simulate the stifling air of long ago. After three turbulent days I went to see Alban.

I swear the year and month are correct -1938, September. The leaves were turning, some had already fallen, I remember them soft and supple from when we sat on the ground for a picnic. The day I saw Alban ride that powerful machine near our house, not far, in fact, from where we lived, I'd made a slight detour with a friend on my way home from school to discuss whether Lottchen could be approached to come cycling with us in the Wiener Wald one afternoon that week. I have a photograph of our outing. The date is on the back, five of us. Lottchen included. Freddie is missing. He took the picture. Our

40

bicycles are stacked against some trees. As I walked up the street and recognized Alban my blood ran cold. He was wearing a Hitler Youth uniform and cut me dead. I've no doubt he'd seen me, for he'd slowed down just about where I was standing, to turn right. He revved the declutched engine several times and then shot off up the street. Between March when the Nazis had arrived and September that year it had become common for us Jews to be cut in the street. Suddenly, people you'd known, as they say, all your life, walked past you as if you didn't exist, making your gesture of greeting look like an idiot's mimicry. We got used to it. But Alban, my cousin, a Nazi? Only a month earlier he'd helped me set up the electric train Uncle Jaques, on one of his rare visits from America, had brought for me. He was Alban's uncle too, my mother's eldest brother, twenty-three years her senior. Martin, Alban's father, had died earlier that year. He'd collapsed on his bike outside the Bourse. That's why Jaques had come, to pay his respects to the family. He was a tall, elegant man with a moustache and sunburnt skin. He wore spats. He was famous in the family because he'd witnessed the holocaust in San Francisco. He'd gone there because as a student he'd incurred some gambling debts which his father had settled in return for Jaques's immediate departure for the United States. During the three years it took to rebuild the City of the Golden Gate, Jaques had amassed a fortune in real estate. On account of his experience everyone always expected him to say incredible things. He didn't, though. I remember my mother prompting him to talk, using her hands and her smile to seduce words to come out of him. But all he came out with was that the bay was blue, real deep blue, and the earthquake - oh, that's so long ago no one ever talks about it nowadays. Supposed to keep the Devil away, he chuckled, keeping his tall back straight. He'd remained a bachelor and special respect was accorded him, a toll everyone paid for possible inclusion in his will.

Alban was older than us, ten years at least, but he liked visiting our house to play with us and build constructions with our Märklin sets and then, after Jaques's visit, to set up the train whose twisting lines and figure eight took up half the floor of my room. Frieda, our maid, cursed it and complained all the time and looked forward to the day we'd take it to pieces again. How could she keep the place clean, and my mother such a stickler for spotlessness? There were veiled threats. Suppose I'd tread on that signal-box or those trees we'd stuck into lumps of plasticine? We weren't on good terms for a while, there were no treats from the kitchen on account of that obstruction on the floor, and we made the train run every day, felt obliged to after all the work Alban had put in, also to invalidate Frieda's constant remonstrations. We must have sensed that Alban wasn't coming any more, for one day we dismantled the train and put the pieces back into their box. That afternoon Frieda gave us a slice of *Linzertorte*.

I told my mother about Alban and his uniform. Father wasn't about, not even in those days. I used to catch a glimpse of him before going to school. Bidding my mother goodbye whilst she was prancing about the bedroom getting dressed or attending to some part of her toilette, he would groan and ask us to come over to his side of the bed, and we would head his hand like a football and allow him to mumble some blessing without his even opening his eyes. He used to get up for lunch and return in the early hours.

At first my mother didn't believe me and screwed up her eyes as she did when I teased her, my favourite expression of hers. But when she saw I wasn't joking she said, I'm not surprised. Martin told us his brother-in-law was in the SS. A friend of Seyss-Inquart since their student days. And Jaques mentioned a photograph on the piano, an SS officer in uniform, that same man, Alban's uncle.

I liked her deductions, was pleased that my sighting of Alban had been the catalyst that had set them in motion. The last Thursday of October we left. It was Frieda's day off and my mother left an envelope with money on the table for her, and a note saying we weren't coming back.

Five years ago I went to Alban's house unannounced like a conquering soldier who needs pay no attention to the niceties of good behaviour. Alban himself opened the door and when he recognized who I was he called out my name with great excitement. They came to the door, Alban's wife, Lothar and Dieter, his two sons and, shuffling behind, Selma, his mother. His wife was the first to talk. 'I thought we'd never meet, never ever. Alban's talked so much about you, so many times, but I said to him, I used to say to him,' she said, raising her finger and touching her pretty face, ' "I don't believe that cousin of yours exists. You're making him up." It's easy to invent families these days, Jewish families in particular, 'cos there's nobody left you can ask whether they knew anyone fifteen or twenty years ago. You hear of so many swindles, people come here and claim they're somebody else in order to get their hands on property that never belonged to them. I used to tell Alban that's what he should do, put in a nice fat claim. Why not? It's the only way he'll ever make any money. Specially after Uncle Jaques's will arrived. Took years to get a copy. Nothing. All that talk for years about a rich uncle. He left the lot to some floozie in New York.'

The nice side of Alban, as of old, was his tolerance. How else could he have stood by in silence to let this woman speak so freely with someone she'd never met in her life? She had blonde hair, cut short, and blue laughing eyes, and a pretty mouth. She'd lost her youthful figure, it showed on her face, her chubby cheeks. She was quite vivacious and interested in flirting, not only with people but with ideas too, and this made her appear a little wild and reckless, unable to be calm. I believe Heidi's sudden outburst was the result of a cooped-up existence.

The old lady inquired about my parents. Her voice had a distant sound which was accentuated by her doll-like immobility as she spoke. Her movements were stiff, she expended sparse energy when she angled her arm to shake my hand. I told her my father had died on the beach and that my mother collected umbrellas. That information shocked and amused her, her mouth twisted, but the decorum of old age stopped her from smiling. And as we went into the room to sit down, the first thing I noticed was that photograph on the upright, a family

43

group, at the centre of which stood a man in SS uniform.

'That was my uncle, my mother's brother,' Alban said when he saw what I was looking at. 'He copped it at Stalingrad. A right number he was.'

Once more I heard that expression my mother used when dismissing a rogue. That picture in its trashy black frame rimmed in faded gold, why had I come to this house? I was in enemy territory, at best on alien ground.

Lothar, the elder son, noticed what I felt. 'Why don't you get rid of that picture? It makes me sick.'

'Lothar,' his mother called out, her voice raised. She'd come back into the room to fetch a silver jug. 'You know Oma won't have it moved, it's the only picture she possesses of her twin brother.'

'I don't care. I don't want to look at that Nazi.'

Lothar, his dark hair short and shiny, was leaning back on the sofa, his foot adangle. Brown eyes.

'Lothar, now please,' Heidi said. She smiled and wasn't in the least angry, in fact was quite proud of her son's rebelliousness. Also it showed her son on her side for a moment, against her husband and that mother of his they all had to tolerate because they were living in her house. Dieter, the younger son, looked pretty. His mother had called him to the kitchen to fetch the tray with cups and saucers. Lothar tried to make him laugh, but Dieter succeeded in reaching the table safely and set the tray down. He then came and sat next to me and whispered to his father, inquiring where I came from. South Africa, he was told.

'South Africa!' Heidi called out, putting down the jug of coffee she was about to pour. 'Africa!' She made it sound like *ta-la-tar*, that cry of Hannibal's men when they saw the sea after their arduous march. 'That must be paradise, all that sun, those beaches and the sea. Oh, how I long for the sun, you've no idea. And the sea! You know, I've never seen the sea? We always go to the mountains and the lakes.'

'And there are many Negroes?' Dieter asked, intoning wonder and fear, that Viennese flavour of exaggeration.

'Idiot,' his brother called him. 'They all run round in bare feet and carry spears.'

'And the women wear nothing?' Dieter went on with his questions, drawing bosoms on his chest. He giggled a bit. 'We've got Negroes in Vienna. In the American army.'

In that first hour at Alban's house an allegiance was formed between Lothar and myself. I felt his assertion, his call for me to be his ally.

The room was drab, the curtains were threadbare in places, lack of money had preserved and worn down every stick of funiture. That worried Heidi.

'That new sofa you've talked about. Alban keeps saying we'll get a new one, but he's all talk. At first he said we couldn't get rid of his mother's furniture, not alter a stitch in this place. Then, as the children grew up - you know what children are like, they ruin everything - I wanted a velvet sofa, gold velvet. You remember, Alban, the one we saw in the Dorotheergasse? What a beauty, fit for a sultan's palace.'

The boys had heard it all before and were laughing, and put their legs across the arms of the sofa. When Heidi saw what they were at she told them to desist and stopped her silly tirade. The old lady, hard of hearing and with nobody talking to her, got up and started to toddle out of the room. Heidi made signs to Alban. Should they stop her? He whispered to her to let her go. I was glad when she left. I wanted them all to go, to be left alone with Alban.

Alban remembered my father cycling with his to Grinzing to drink wine, both in knickerbockers, my father at least a head taller than his. When his father had died, mine had stopped coming to their house, Alban didn't know why. His mother, he said, was never easy to get on with.

'Perhaps', I said, 'that fellow on the piano stopped his Aryan sister from mixing with Jews? I imagine he had something to do with it, and your joining the Hitler Youth.'

'The Hitler Youth?'

'I saw you one day in full regalia on your motor bike.'

'I take it that's a joke?'

45

'I saw you as close as I am now.'

'Not me.'

His calm made me feel a fool. All those years I'd been convinced of what I'd seen, and now I heard his denial. It was best not to believe him. I'd seen since I'd arrived that acquiescent side of his, that tolerance I'd so much admired as a boy when he'd set up that train in my room. Now that Heidi of his was hounding him, she'd scream all the way as the rat of ageing gnawed at her, whilst his mother domineered in silence, ruling her wretched domain aided by that dead twin on the upright. Alban was weak. I'd mistaken his weakness for tolerance.

'Early in 1940 I went into hiding on a farm near St Wolfgang. My mother's people. That place by the lake with its famous inn was a haven for Nazis. They all gathered there, and they told me at the farm it wasn't safe there any longer, not for them or me. If they caught a half-Jew, what was left of him after they'd finished with him they sent down the road to Dachau. I made for France, a nightmare of a hike, I can tell you, then crossed the Pyrenees into Spain and worked in a cellar at Haro pumping wine.'

I wasn't convinced. To this day I can't tell whether facts are true or false. You remember that snapshot of our picnic? Freddie was missing because he took the photograph. Someone told me they saw Freddie taken away in '41, and he never came back. He's missing again, this time for good. If I can't believe what I know, my sanity cracks. I know that noise. I can hear it better than most, like rats that rush from underground passages before the ground caves in. Alban was lying. He had reason to lie, to keep his bent past from his sons. Did Heidi know? She'd sell her support for being allowed to badger him, to throw her flirtatious tantrums, to make noises about her expectations, and all the louder the more her ambitions became thwarted. And his mother, he could keep her in check. If ever she'd blurt out the truth he could deny it by hitting her with her age. What fantasies she came out with! There was a cat in her room, she'd said one day, and then Heidi had pointed to her

46

long fingernails she'd not cut for ten days, so whenever she picked up her hairbrush and knife and fork she'd made a scraping noise. The way to get rid of the truth is to live the lie.

Five

I've forgotten to mention Lothar's leg. The right one is damaged, the aftermath of infantile paralysis. Seeing it for the first time gave me a shock, but then I soon forgot about it. His strides have robot quality and he gets angry if you slow down on his account, or avoid difficult passages. He can't run. I was wondering whether to mention it at all, and then decided to because it helps delineate his character with more precision. He never complains about his leg.

Alban is dead. A tumour on the brain. Two years ago Lothar sent me a short note about it. It was amongst a bundle of letters Frau Eppstein had collected whilst I had a spell in a madhouse on the outskirts of London. I didn't feel much when I read about Alban's death, in fact I was surprised at my callous indifference. Because over the last ten years I've not been well so many times, I'm never certain whether what I feel is true, whether I'm out of the storm or heading for new disaster. I have good periods in between, calm and clarity, beautiful days. And then Alban's mother died a year later. That note from Lothar announcing her death made me feel good, particularly as he said that at last they'd got rid of that photograph on the piano. Somehow this news lifted a veil of depression from my mind. I remember quite clearly rubbing my eyes afterwards, as if I'd walked through a cobweb in the Wiener Wald. He pleaded for me to come to Vienna, and as I had no one at that time to keep me in London, I went.

I tried not to stay in the same pension as before so as not in any way to put down roots in a place whence I'd once been deracinated. Somehow, though, I ended up there, in the same room even. I didn't like that, but it was dreadfully hot and I felt too sluggish to find somewhere else. The room had no pleasant memories for me. I'd not come across any girl I wanted to be with, and was prevented, I now remember, from looking for one out of fear and a stifling shyness to reveal my circumcision in this hostile city. Soon after I'd arrived, there was a knock at the door. It was Lothar come to fetch me.

'How did you know I'd stay here?' I asked.

'I knew you would.'

It was the answer I would have given to anyone inquisitive about my cunning. I share with my brother the ability to sense the movement of others. It's something I have always presumed to have inherited from my father, stemming from the luck of conception, that one sperm of his pack hitting my mother's ovum to make the two of us. Later on, in his poker days, that pack was fifty-two cards, the ones to make his hand paid for by a bet. A lethargy hung over the sweltering city, the kids had taken over, they'd been given a few schillings to go swimming and stay out. They took to the stifling heat as if that were the temperature of a new generation, whilst my cousin made for the same place as where I'd stayed before, for the easiest passage is some kind of home-coming. He knew what time the Ostend–Vienna Express arrived at the Westbahnhof, and forty minutes later he knocked at my door.

'I don't live at home any longer, I've got my own place,' Lothar said, blurting this out as an excuse for his sudden arrival. 'My mother's gone mad. Why don't you ever write?' he asked.

There was complaint in his voice, and rightly so. It is unfair how often I had thought of him and not made contact over the last three years except for that scribbled note to say I was coming. There is a reason, it's the way my life goes, and I allow its flow to conduct me. At times I avoid revealing anything to anyone, at others I talk freely to the nearest Harry. Lothar knows nothing of my ups and downs, the weeks and months I've spent in bins, and I don't want him to know, not here in Vienna. Strange that in this city I detest, that gnarled and unctuous dialect they speak, where the truth, you feel, hasn't a chance to live longer than a day - oh, I could go on pouring insults from a bottomless bag I carry in my head to litter every Gasse of this place, I want a clean bill of health, for my head to be as sound as when I started out from here, for don't you give me that crap, Herr fucking Jung, that everything is there in the first three weeks of your life (or is it months?), the fissures are simply widened and made more painful by future hurts. That is not so. You never had it bad, little Gustav, you never had your balls touched by some fat Nazi in the tram. I stood no higher than his belt with that ugly buckle on his belly, he stank of the leather of his boots, the car was crowded and there were beads of sweat on his white face. I felt the language disintegrate in my mouth. Nothing, I tell you, prepared me for such insults when I was born.

The knocks of the last three years had left their mark on Lothar's face. One is told that orphans often inherit some feature of their parent, or take over one of their habits, but that was not so with him. The contrary, in fact. There was none of Alban's softness about the mouth, or that languid hold of the arm, that altogether touch of the American South about his person which Alban's natural propensity had picked up from members of the US Office of Occupation where he'd worked as a clerk. Lothar was tough as steel, there was energy stored up in him. He was not, you could see, easy to deal with. If you wanted what he had, you'd pay his price, which was pitched to exact value.

'We'll walk. It's not far,' he said.

There was nowhere to sit down in my room, only a fragile chair by the bed for my clothes at night, so for a moment he had sat on the bed and, because of its height from the ground, his stiff leg stuck out at an angle which shortly made his hip hurt. I swear that before I locked my room as we went out I knew that he'd move to the Judengasse. It was one of those cunning deductions I made.

'You living alone?' I asked.

'Yes. My girl-friend comes only at night.'

'That's not living alone,' I said.

'We sleep in one bed, that's all. And that's not living together.'

We walked up the Rotenturm Strasse, walked slowly because I knew he wanted to talk before we got to his place.

'I feel I belong here but that nobody knows why I do,' he said.

And then I committed a little indiscretion by laughing aloud. We'd stopped, and he looked at me quizzically, watching my concentration veer to my mother's favourite shop-window. We were right in front of it. The rows of umbrellas, particularly in this heat, looked like desiccated birds on some Habsburg parade.

'Here on this spot,' I declaimed, 'my mother's obsession began, that *ur*-feeling rose in that innocent cow as she was chewing her cud. Suddenly it rained and anchovies started to swim about her auburn hair. Water poured down her face, she tried to lick it with her tongue, and then someone – who that man was, she never found out – held a black umbrella over her to shelter her from the rain. He pulled out a white handkerchief and gave it to her and she dried herself and handed it back to him. He smiled. The downpour stopped.'

I wanted to go on about the umbrellas, how much à la mode they were, how safe you felt under them, they're a roof over your head. But I couldn't continue because people had started to listen, and I was frightened they might whisper things I'd not said and call the police. That had happened to me before, with unpleasant consequences. We went on down the road.

I knew the Jewish quarter, and knew why Lothar had moved there. There are primitive instincts which direct our migration.

'Bambi, my girl, we quarrel a lot,' he said. When he walked every few steps he twisted his mouth as if to expel some overflow of pain. 'That's how she gets her kicks.'

The house had a narrow façade. He unlocked the door and told me nobody else was living there. He showed me the room

51

downstairs where they cooked and ate, but we didn't go in. It was clean and tidy, everything was new. One floor above was where he spent his time. That room was sumptuous with comforts, sofas and chairs, a desk and two cupboards for books, the shelves half-empty.

I asked him, 'Did Alban leave you provided for?'

He laughed. He'd made for the swivel chair and turned it so as to sit facing me. 'Not a schilling,' he said. 'Heidi gets a pension from the Americans and manages on that. He had no money at all. Nor had Oma. She left nothing either.'

'Except that photograph on the piano,' I said, a joke to lift gloom off the subject.

He was suddenly silent. I sensed the portcullis come down to protect the inhabitants of his fortress, and was stranded outside, left to his mercy. I really am strong. At times I can run as fast as a Hollywood chase, scale walls and climb roof-tops and beat my pursuers. At others I'm fixed like that frog by the snake I once saw in the zoo, an image of terror I've carried in my head ever since. I see like a voyeur, everything around me is alive, my universe vibrates with movement and flickering lights, but I am dumb and speechless, miles away from help. For a moment I thought that the heat of the city had raised my temperature to fever point. Lothar was moving on his roving chair, tapping the sides perhaps to avoid looking at me and catching my stare, or else to suggest the swivelling lights which lit up the barbed-wire fence of the concentration camps, a warning to inmates. Thank God fear is a fickle companion and doesn't remain with one long. I'd saved my allowance for three months whilst I was in the bin, and for once had not gone on a spree when I came out. Having funds in hand made me feel good. That's what I was thinking about when Lothar broke the silence.

'I took that photograph from the piano when Oma died. I'd planned it all. I was going to burn it and throw the ashes into the Donau to let that Nazi float out of my life. But on the back of it I found a map which no one had seen before, and that's why we are going to St Wolfgang. We'll leave within the hour and get there by nightfall and we'll stay by the lake. I know that lake. I've been there several times. That map shows the lake with arrows pointing near the edge, just outside the village.'

'You think there's Nazi gold?'

'Maybe.'

'Where was that picture taken?'

'In Kretschmar's garden at Linz. Oma always talked about her brother's neat little garden with its English lawn. I've suspected for a long time that Kretschmar is still alive. A strong hunch. I don't believe he died at Stalingrad. Members of the SS disappeared to survive, and Stalingrad was a useful ploy.'

'You think he's still alive?'

'Could be. I've been waiting for him to appear ever since Oma died. We put it in the papers, a nice big announcement with a thick black border. A lot of our top Nazis were sentimental slobs, and I thought his sister's death might make him come out of hiding. I'd like to ask him about that map and then slam the door in his face.'

Lothar, I could see, had gone mad. He'd cottoned on to those rumours, rife since the end of the war, that the Nazis had hidden treasure in the Austrian lakes. He must have known more, though, than he was telling me. He was living in style, his house was expensively decorated, carpets and curtains, everything was to a fine finish. How had he amassed enough money to pay for all this? He'd not volunteered to tell me. Vienna was always a place for unsavoury deals. Art, I'd heard, was smuggled from the East, icons by the score. There was a brisk trade in jewellery which refugees from Russia sold for next to nothing to get some Western currency. All kinds of bargains were struck by unscrupulous dealers which left them with rich pickings. But Lothar was not one of those. He didn't fit the image of the importuning tout tackling weary Russian Jews as they stepped penniless into freedom. You could see them, that verminous gathering of hucksters, hours before the train arrived from the East, ready to pounce with flattering words of welcome before stating their business. Drugs came to mind, it's a clean and profitable business. I'd bought from pushers and knew Jose

Maria Da Silva well. He was Sabatine's favourite in the Cit de Coeur, bought Madame flowers every Friday. When the police plucked him from his first-floor apartment they found six pounds of the white powder, and boxes filled with other marketable goodies. He'd been a student at Coimbra and had got into trouble with Salazar's strong men for painting slogans on the wall. At Auschwitz they played Bach at executions. That was a German dish. Somehow I associate that Iberian pusher with those executions, for he used to read Camoens and translate it for me line by line, beautifully, with great passion, whilst allowing me to sniff whatever I could get up my nose. What did Lothar do?

He went off to get his pyjamas and took Bambi's toothbrush for me and then we left to fetch his car from the garage. Ten minutes later we were on the road.

I can't drive, and when being driven I am stunned by the manoeuvres of the driver, his skills of judgement and the obedient response of the vehicle under his control. For a time my admiration for the driver fetters me and I enjoy the sensation of moving at speed a foot or so off the ground, but it soon wears off and I start feeling frightened and pick up engine odours. How can you tell every nut and bolt will hold fast, the tyres hold air, and I swallow saliva in gulps until my brow cools and I feel once more at ease. Lothar drove well, I could sense his confidence, but I suspected him to be reckless on account of his leg and the weird purpose of our trip. It was good to have got away from the stifling city, though the heat, quite frankly, had not bothered me that much, as I was used to African temperatures. And then, perhaps because I'd raced in one second to Africa and saw myself as astronauts see the earth as they lift into space, I suddenly knew that Lothar carried a gun. More, if you like, of my cunning. I opened the glove compartment and saw it lying there.

'Just in case,' Lothar said, grinning. 'We're going to dangerous parts. The lakes are notorious for murder. Every month you read about some floater being dragged ashore.'

He drove at great speed and overtook everything in front of

us, and the concentration required for this somehow absolved Lothar from speaking to me. I'd never in my life touched a revolver, and seeing this murderous weapon lie not two feet in front of me, neatly wedged between maps, with its shiny black handle facing me, I became almost high, the nausea of the drive was replaced by a different terror.

'Pull it out and take a look, but watch the safety-catch.'

Why am I always stunned by surprise and pushed into abject inactivity? I should have wound the window down and thrown out that weapon to deflate the explosive atmosphere inside the car. But I didn't. As I reached for the gun not even Lothar's warning that it was loaded stopped me from getting hold of it and feeling its cool butt in my palm. I wish I'd never touched that lethal instrument. I knew the moment I put my finger on the trigger that I was hooked, that one day I'd want to use it.

We reached St Wolfgang by nightfall. The lake was silent, the water very still. Lakes at night are nurseries when children have gone to bed. There's suddenly no life, the birds have withdrawn to their nests, boats are tied to moorings. The water is in charge, some mothering spirit guards that wet domain, even the moonlight brushing the water is kept out. We saw some shimmering stripes, its cold reflection. I much prefer the sea to those holes in the earth filled with water.

Lothar knew his way about. He'd driven right through the village past the White Horse Inn and we'd come along the water's edge to the Pension Tyrol. It's the last house at the end of that road, a rustic structure with wooden eaves and shuttered windows. Guests were still eating on the veranda along the front. The landlord, Sep, followed us in and offered us rooms at the back. He called out Helga several times, in rising crescendo, and when after the third call Helga had still not appeared, he called her a slut and shouted her name once more. It's common enough in Austria to shout at servants. For a moment I expected Louise to appear. Helga was pretty.

'My daughter will show you to your rooms,' Sep said. 'And then you'd better come down to eat.'

On the way up Helga told us where there was dancing that

night and where later on she'd be drinking a glass or two with friends. Come along. How friendly she was, how pretty and inviting! She had the best pair of legs I'd seen in years and the prettiest mouth. I watched her go downstairs and heard her father shout for her to come at once. She took little notice, in fact she stopped when she heard him, to preen herself in front of the mirror on the landing.

We were the last to be served with goulash and noodles. A few guests were finishing their beers and then got up to walk to the village, all of them I noticed, and I remarked on this to Lothar.

'There's nothing the other way. A footpath, it soon gets steep, no one goes there at night. There've been quite a few accidents. To the right the road stops after two hundred metres.'

Sep, a glass in his hand, came to our table. He inquired about the heat wave in Vienna and told us how pleasant the weather was in St Wolfgang. There was a new moon, that's why it was so dark that night. The way Lothar had driven to the Pension, had known exactly where to go, made me think he'd stayed there before. Sep knew of the Kretschmars, where Alban had stayed when he'd been on the run, didn't know them personally but knew where their farm was, up on the hill, left on the road to Salzburg. 'But him,' Sep said, meaning me but looking at Lothar, 'I could swear I've seen him before. But where?' he asked himself, knocking his forehead lightly with his fist.

'It's my first time here,' I told Sep. I knew the moment I'd spoken that that aroused his suspicion even more.

'I'll think of it, it'll come back,' he said, lowering his hand. 'Then I'll tell you. Funny people, those Kretschmars.' He wanted to know more from Lothar, who now, I was sure, regretted having mentioned their name. 'Friends of yours?'

'They have a special breed of goats, someone in my department told me. I do research on enzymes in cheese.'

Sep went off-beam but wasn't convinced by Lothar's way out. I, however, was proud of him. Quite a convincing lie, I thought, but how long can you lie in a place where everyone

56

knows each other? The veranda was empty but for the two of us and Sep. Even Helga had gone. She'd left through the back to avoid her father's abuse. He'd gone in to close the ledgers for the day or to phone his contacts in the village. Two strangers have arrived who know the Kretschmars. Everyone this side of the lake would be on the look-out for us.

'We'll take the car,' Lothar said, after we'd decided to go down to the village. 'My leg is tired.'

It was the first time he'd pointed to a weakness in his leg. I was glad. I cursed the lake's soft surface for hemming us in, limiting our chance of escape. I felt safe in the car, the gun within reach.

'Give it to me,' Lothar said, pointing to it. He put the revolver inside his trousers, he had a pocket for it there, the side of his gammy leg. He stopped not far from Die Krone, where Helga had invited us to join her.

Strange the contrasts you come across when you're afraid. You expect the tap on the shoulder, the barrel of a gun at your back, shadows conceal your attacker. You're stiff with fright, dead if you like. When we opened the door of the inn the noise was deafening. There are long tables in Austrian taverns. You sit next to strangers and talk God knows what about and join in the songs led by a sinister band of minstrels. Night after night they play the same songs. We looked for Helga and spotted her all right. So friendly she was, she waved to us to come over and pushed the men either side of her to move over, so as to make room for us. It was awkward for Lothar to push his leg across the bench, but he managed. Come on, push, someone said that end of the table. Can't you see the young man is a cripple? He was trying to be helpful and Lothar acknowledged his concern. They'll imagine, I thought, that that hard thing at his side is part of his truss. Helga, who'd redone her face before she'd come out, ordered wine from the waiter for us. We were, I should think, ten years younger at least than the men who sat next to her. The one at my side had a good face, classical features, straight nose, blue eyes, a well-proportioned chin. Until he opened his mouth. When he spoke, his lips, I noticed, went sideways, and the lower one trembled at vowels, and those tremors pointed to a cruelty you'd not have suspected from looking at him. Helga had talked about us, or had it been Sep?

'From Vienna, are you?'

I said yes, and told him for some years I'd lived in Africa. My German was good, too good for a foreigner, but sometimes I stumbled into English. I told them about Africa to allay future suspicion.

'Eight dead from the heat in Vienna, they said on the radio, and there'll be more before it's over. People in cities don't know how to cope with heat.'

I'm dumbfounded by strangers and never know what to say. Someone across the table took up his theme and told us that when it gets hot the cattle move higher up the hills.

I was so close to Helga I could hardly see her, except for her face and hands. I hate picking up details I'd rather stay clear of. The light was unkind, the heat in the place played tricks with her skin. I don't know what I was about examining her blemishes, black lines on her coarse fingers, some twists of hair on her chin, coarse little tufts. The bodice of her dirndl was low and she'd undone the top button, and though the skin above her breasts was smooth, her neck was quite rough. I look for and find blemishes when I stand little chance with a woman.

I don't know what began the argument, I had missed the beginning, but as soon as the banter started to criss-cross the length of our table I knew we'd been selected as targets for attack. I tried to catch Lothar's attention, but he was parrying words with the man who'd called him a cripple, and Helga took hold of my hand whilst she joined in Lothar's defence. That drunken, gluttonous peasant who was shouting at Lothar, you could see a haze of vaporous venom ooze from his rough face.

'So you've come for Kramer's goats?' he shouted.

There was sudden silence. I had no way, with Helga between us, of asking Lothar about those wretched goats – how had he known about them, was his lie constructed on fact? Did they actually exist? They'd come round with more beer and wine. That broke the silence which, I noticed, had made Lothar take

58

his arm off the table, surreptitiously, I imagined, to put his hand in his pocket to feel the gun.

'A prize herd of goats. A Nubian breed black as Sudanese niggers.'

'And their milk', Lothar said, 'is whiter than that of any cow.'

'The purest in the world,' someone said.

There seemed to be a general knowledge of goats. Goats, they told us, were domesticated by the prehistoric inhabitants of the Austrian lakes. That's where Kramer got his idea of breeding his famous herd.

'Pure Aryan goats!'

'Kramer's SS,' someone said.

This rang like a whiplash through the crowd and once more there was that electric silence. Everyone was frightened. They'd gone too far, that's the impression I had. There was something about Kramer they didn't want to tell. Keep strangers out! Perhaps there was something planned, some feud set to erupt, mysterious events occur in mountain regions. I had no idea what it was, and terror adds to confusion. And then, suddenly, I thought of that map Lothar had shown me on the back of his uncle's picture which he'd folded up with sharp creases to begin its destruction, and I wondered whether that was the key they'd all been waiting for for years and which we, by weird circumstance, had brought to St Wolfgang. Someone - I saw the nod, it was Franzl who seemed to be in charge, he'd done most of the talking so far - gave the sign to go on with Kramer.

'It's all so long ago, Franzl, why . . .'

'Tell them!' he shouted. He banged his fist on the table and was lucky, I thought, to find an empty space amongst all the glasses in front of him. He wanted to be asked to tell the story himself, and that's what happened.

'It *is* a long time ago, and Kramer left here and didn't come back till many years after the war. And since he's come back we've hardly caught sight of him. People say he's changed a great deal and that he talks to no one.'

'Only to his goats.'

'He even changed his name when he got back, to Kretschmar.

His wife had stayed here all the time, a nice enough woman, she still occasionally comes to the village. There were a number of murders at the beginning of the war. People looked for a chance to settle old scores, and murder is not uncommon in these parts. Down a ravine, they were, not far from here. A shepherd, who was looking for some lost sheep, found them. He found the frozen corpses of several young Jews. The cold rocks had preserved them perfectly. They looked, it was said, as if they'd been dead for only a few hours. There were burns all over them, circular marks where the skin had turned black, and everyone knew whose branding-iron had been used. There was a K where the hot iron had gone deep to mark the flesh. It was Gauleiter Kramer's mark. When kids are three days old they use a disbudding iron to treat their horns. Goats fight. That's why they blunt their horns.'

The fellow who'd first been instructed by Franzl to tell the story now carried on.

'They arrested the shepherd and then he disappeared during Kramer's reign of terror that followed. No one was safe any longer.'

'That was a good change of name,' somebody said. 'He didn't even have to change the initial on his cuff-links!'

Someone gripped my shoulder and pushed me to one side. It was Sep, who'd arrived to join the party. He squeezed his daughter's thigh to make her jump, a moment he used to gain more room and make the others move. Franzl was glad to see him. He needed an ally his age our end of the table.

The more I wanted to talk to Lothar, one word would have sufficed, the further we were driven apart, now by Sep's arrival. I could not even see his face, make out what affect that story we'd just heard had had on him, what he was likely to say.

'I remember Kramer boasting that there wasn't a Jew left in our part of the world. He'd stopped them building a camp this side of Salzburg. We want clean air, he said, the nearest yids are in Dachau. That's near enough.'

'I remember that.'

'Anyone looking suspicious had his trousers pulled down.'

60

'And God help anyone whose foreskin was missing!'

'What about yours?' Sep suddenly asked me. 'Let's have a look at it.' He banged the table with his big flat hand. 'Put it there.'

I laughed at him, the best laugh I could muster. 'I'll show your daughter later, if she likes.' What repartee! There were roars of laughter. I said *bore pri hagofim*, the Jew's blessing for wine, though nobody heard. No matter the brute strength of this company, I'd outwit them all. I'd sat there without saying a word the whole time, and suddenly they'd made me the hero of the table. Helga smiled and waved her finger at me. That produced catcalls all around the table, until someone said it was time to go.

The place had emptied and I'd not realized we were the last to get up. It was good to stand once more next to Lothar, a closeness I'd missed for the past hour or so. It was late, but Sep was discussing with several of our company where we could go on drinking. The village was dead. Nothing was open there. Our only chance, Franzl said, was Das Fuchsl. That was open late. Not every night, someone said. If they're open we'll see the light from the distance.

Only Franzl and Sep were keen on the trip. The others went off into the night, and I was frightened that Helga too might go off and leave us alone with our strange companions, so I folded my arm in hers and made her laugh by telling her I'd not let go of her that night. She came with us and sat at the back with Sep and myself.

Franzl in front gave directions to Lothar. 'It's over that hill,' he said when after a few minutes we came to open country. 'Go left up there, the road's a bit bumpy. It's a short cut.'

I don't know why Lothar followed these instructions without a word of objection. That road was rough. The car with its heavy load scraped over boulders, there was suddenly a mass of stones in front of us.

'Keep to the left,' Franzl said, holding on to the door-handle.

And that's exactly what Sep was doing as well, riding in the back with his hand on the door-lever. He'd whispered

61

something to his daughter, but she was suddenly overcome with fear for her own safety - she'd struck her head on the roof of the car - and called out that we were on the wrong track and for God's sake turn back at once before it was too late.

That's the instruction Lothar followed.

The next morning we went to inspect exactly where we'd stopped that night and saw a gaping quarry with a drop of two hundred feet. We decided at once to leave the Pension Tyrol, paid our bill and made for Kramer's farm.

Six

I've raced to put the events of that night down on paper. When we got back to our rooms we were overcome by the fatigue that saps the hunted. We slept behind locked doors, my sleep had a soundness that has stayed in my memory. In fact I remarked on it when I talked to Lothar the next morning. We'd had, he said, our nightmares before going to bed. That's why we'd slept as heavily as men condemned to death. I remember his smile when he said that.

Lothar had samurai qualities. He'd appear at times to be absent from events so as to hold himself ready to grip his sword for that accurate, practised cut. You could never know when you'd come to that moment of surprise when he'd reveal some new fact you felt he'd kept back. It was something, quite often, he'd known for years, and stuck until it was needed into the gun-belt of his memory. 'Kramer,' he said. 'Papa never told us. He knew about those goats. He knew everything.'

I wanted that moment to hold Lothar in my arms, his face looked so sad I wanted to comfort him, to hold his hand. Taboo, Herr Jung, held me back.

'It's a secret he kept to save honour,' Lothar went on, 'not to bring shame to his mother. But now Oma is dead that's not an inheritance I have to take on. I'll go there.'

That's what he said, and I wondered for a moment whether he intended to exclude me from his visit. Nothing, I felt, could stop him. He had that look in his eyes which overcomes pain, all

63

kinds of rubbish surfaced at that fermenting moment. How could that wound be healed, that branded K poisoning his blood which made him fester, how could that scream for revenge die down like fading echoes? I was frightened of the gun in his pocket, I knew it was there, that he'd not be without it now.

The road rose high above the lake. I wanted to see the view but did not dare turn round. To occupy my mind in my frenzied calm I thought of superstitions and abided by their laws, Sodom below us in that haze. I refused to look. The girl who'd given food to that Sodomite stranger for which they'd bound her and painted her face with honey. They'd left her lying in the sun for the bees to eat her flesh. I looked for her on that drive to Kramer's farm. The gate looked dangerous and Lothar wore gloves to open the latch in case of electric currents. A sign *Beware of Dogs* flanked the inner gate. By now someone must have heard us, our engine was in low gear as we climbed the final incline to the house. The pens with Kramer's goats were at the back, beyond a row of rocks. The air was clean.

No one came to the door. The downstairs windows were shut. At the top I saw one that was open. The chimney was dead. Perhaps because of those precious beasts no smoke was allowed to blacken the air. A bird's feather, having dropped warm in flight, had stuck to one of the steps. In quest, I suppose, of some sound, I looked for birds, but there wasn't one I could see on that treeless hillside. Then, at the back, we heard a dog, its footsteps and its pumping breaths. It came closer, then no further. Someone had the dog on a leash. A woman appeared whom Lothar assumed to be Kramer's wife. He held out his hand. 'I'm Lothar,' he said. 'Alban's son.'

She was caught unawares and wiped her hand across her face. Then she feebly shook Lothar's hand. She was old, her hair was lifeless and white. I thought I heard a stifled shriek when Lothar mentioned his father's name, but I couldn't swear whether this was so or simply my expectation. Beyond where she stood and those mumbled words was trespass, that's why she'd made no move to bid us welcome. Lothar told her my name and pointed to me at his back. I'd moved and made him turn a bit too far so that he nearly fell over, and then she noticed his awkward leg for the first time and became a little less timid. Not many words had been spoken, nor had the dog growled, but in that isolation the noise we'd made had caused a commotion and I saw the curtain of one of the downstairs windows move. It must have been the man we'd come to see, for no one else, I suspected, was living in that house.

'What do you want?' the woman asked, as if to retract her acknowledgement of Lothar.

'We've come to see Kramer, my father's uncle. My grand-mother was Selma, Herr Kramer's sister.'

'Herta!' a voice suddenly called from the house. That call was repeated, louder. Herta turned to go and answer, and was gone for some time whilst Lothar and I waited, too dumbfounded to speak. The front door opened with hardly any sound, and Kramer stood there. From where we saw him, outlined by the door frame, he looked much like that figure in the photograph, so much so that at first I looked for that dreaded armband on his uniform. He was tall. His black coat had a military cut and he wore high boots, a left-over from former days. It was strange, after all that time one had seen him in that photo, to hear him speak.

'My sister's dead. My wife told me. Young Alban ran off in the war. In the village they found out about him and threw him out of the Hitler Youth. He had to go.'

At the doorstep of this alpine house, Lothar heard the truth about his father. All his life Alban had lied, had thought, like his uncle, that no witness would ever turn up to uncover his past. I'd seen him in his regalia all right.

'Used to help me with my beasts, young Alban. He was in charge of the bucks, and he fed them well. There are only six for the entire herd, the purest breed in the world, black as night.'

He went on for some time about his beasts, how the strain was kept pure, how the weaklings were killed a few days after they were born, together with the young bucks. 'Such tasty white meat,' he said.

'You can't eat them all,' Lothar said. 'I suppose you throw

65

some of them down a ravine and let them rot there?'

'We bury them,' he said. He wanted to show us his herd, but before stepping out of the house he suddenly asked, 'And Alban, what happened to him?'

'He's dead,' Lothar said.

The old man then became quite lively, the feigning of old age disappeared, he stepped out into the sun and led the way.

'I suppose', Lothar said when Kramer turned round and saw him limp, 'you'd have killed me if I'd been one of your goats?'

'Most likely.'

He laughed, and then led us on.

When we came to the pens, there must have been two hundred goats, Kramer led us straight to the bucks. Unusually big they were, taller than all the rest. 'My beauties,' he said. 'The fathers of the herd.'

Why Kramer didn't grasp what Lothar was up to I have no idea. He was stunned when Lothar fired the first shot, when the beast heaved over and fell to the ground. Then he suddenly knew we'd come for revenge, he made noises he must often have heard before, perhaps long ago, but unforgettable enough. There are no tears in old men's eyes, else he would have wept.

When the last of the bucks fell dead Lothar took out the photograph and tore it up. 'On the back,' he told Kramer, though it is doubtful if he heard what was said, 'my father drew that ravine with arrows pointing to those murdered Jews.'

Then we left the old fool.

* * *

Seven

Book Two starts with the following entry:

* * *

I am steaming, for two reasons. The first is that I am cold. It's been freezing for the past ten days, and Sabatine thinks the Seine will ice up any day, if not this week then *sûrement* the next. Of all the times of the year why is Maman late with my remittance so that I can't even buy fuel for our stove? To make matters worse, Annie's parents have discovered that she's been cheating, they've spotted her in Paris when she was supposed to be in London, and now they won't give her a bean. The other day her father caught her outside Notre-Dame, and within the precincts of that holy place he threatened to beat the daylights out of her. That night, sensing financial difficulties looming in the distance, the two directors of our bank - Annie, that is, and myself - sat down and held a crisis meeting. We made a list of friends and acquaintances from whom we might borrow a few francs, then made a rather pretty sort of advent calendar with only, alas, seven little windows, on which we'd written the number of francs we might ask for, plus the name of our potential benefactor. The figures were small, from ten to forty francs. Now all those windows are open and that calendar hangs like a skull by the window and stares at me. And still no money from that sweltering cow rollicking in the sun. That's

67

reason one why I'm steaming. It's my breath hitting the cold air. Reason two is a violent argument I had with Annie. Da Silva lets us use his bath downstairs, and last night was our bath-night. Annie was to go down first and she asked me if she should leave the water in. As a rule I like washing in water that has enveloped her, it is an increase of touching that pleases me. But for three weeks now she's been evading me, and in spite of all remonstrances to the contrary I know this to be true. Gone is that girlish happiness, that softness about the mouth and eyes which were there at the moment of submission, when both of us, that is, submitted to each other. Now it's only I chasing some sack of flesh I pierce open to let my prick enter the soft flower of her body, and that's not enough. It drives me wild and I feel robbed of peace. Instead of satisfying my obsession with her it nurtures it, and I suspect every move she makes, every step she takes, every word she speaks. When she smokes the stuff she becomes more mellow, more her old self. But now I don't smoke much because I have to stay alert to keep my eye on her. I've even developed a trick of playing with the muscle of my cheek-bone which keeps my ear strained so that I can hear the faintest nuance in her speech. So when she asked me last night whether to leave the water in, I told her to pull the plug out to let her menstruating pollution drain away. I know it's that time of the month, but that's never bothered me before, nor her. 'And what's more,' I shouted after her, 'clean the fucking tub when you get out!' And, quite beside myself, I called her a whore. That's reason two why I'm steaming.

I must say this morning I look a sight. Da Silva had gone out, so we could spend as long as we liked in his bath. I lay in there for quite some time, adding more hot when the water cooled off. His razor lay on the shelf and I picked it up, I don't quite know why, though I suspect now I was following Annie's movements when she was doing her ablutions. I know she'd used his soap, for the cake was lying in a little pool of water and there were still bubbles on it. And that razor was sitting in a place that spanned to Annie's reach exactly. I touched it like a tec touching the bonnet of a car to feel if it's still warm. It

68

wasn't, of course, for metal quickly cools. But there were hairs stuck to the blade, not from Da Silva's beard but from Annie's legs. So she kept herself trim, that bitch, though not, I swear, for me. She'd been out a good deal that month, the last week, she said, to get warm, just walking about, traipsing the Parisian boulevards. I then took Da Silva's hand-mirror and started to shave my head. I'd done a quarter of it when I decided to go the whole hog. After that I watched my shorn hair float on the water, forming a map no stranger than that of the world, and no less arbitrarily put together. So what? I took another look at myself and, as I gripped the mirror, saw that my nails were long and now soft enough to cut without much difficulty. There were scissors to hand so I started to cut as much as I could reach. That way, Mummy, no dirt can come between me and my nails. The thought of Irma in my nakedness, believe it or not, led me to my eyebrows. The more I can destroy of myself, I thought, the greater the insult to her creation. So off I shaved my eyebrows, and now I looked really plucked, like one of those slaughtered chickens in the yard my mother orders to be cremated for the table. Annie shrieked when I came up, and then laughed and laughed - oh, that laughter was worth all the shearing, and we rolled into bed, my body still warm from the bath. Ah, when she touched my bare head, why had I ever let my hair grow?

I woke up in the middle of the night. Even when I'm heavily doped I never sleep through, and lately I've found that broken sleep stands in my favour. I watch Annie sleep and watch over her, which makes me feel her guardian, her protector, and this gives me strength to lie at times in some cramped position so as not to disturb her, until it strains a muscle so much that the pain becomes unbearable, and all this I suffer because of that immemorial role of the male which makes me protect my companion. When Annie turns in her sleep, she turns her entire body, expands the energy that's required for such twists, and doesn't notice who's lying next to her! It is I who only a few hours ago made you play those delightful tunes on your pipes! When she turns over I swear she pushes me away, as if she were fighting for the frontiers of her privacy, breaking the alliance we'd enjoyed after my bath. I felt cold. My head, I tell you, I screwed my hand from under the blanket to touch it, felt cold. The skylight of our attic picks up some of the street light, and thus the unchanging light throughout the night blocks the passage of time and makes the night longer. I don't understand why she can't read me as I can read her. Put your sleeping hand, my love, faithless on my shaven head, please. But nothing happens and I stare unheard at the sloping roof of our attic. Not a good night.

In the morning Annie was already dressed when she brought me a mug of tea, and we hardly spoke. She smiled at me on account of my head and called me crazy boy. She's gone out and won't be back till late afternoon. She'll bring some food for a meal. God knows where she's gone.

Apropos of goats, Marie-Claire told me an amusing story when I saw her at La Laterne. Twice weekly she visits that bordel in the Rue Bonaparte and lectures charmingly on artists who've drawn their inspiration from these houses of pleasure. And what an appropriate setting she's chosen, for I doubt if there is anywhere in the world a more satisfactory place in which to lounge about in the attire of your choice, or, for that matter, naked, for these plush rooms are always adequately heated so as to be conducive, unlike this freezing attic, to carnal pleasure. Many famous artists have visited there, or are said to have frequented the place, for there is no doubt that art and a brothel have in common pure desire and the urge to satisfy it. More often than not, we well know, satisfaction escapes us but that does not prevent thousands from visiting bordels every day of the year, or filling canvases with limp rubbish. I first went there when I was in a state so high that every door was open to me, though when Madame Rose inquired as to exactly what pleasure I wished to procure, I was too dumbfounded to answer her. She wastes little time and after a minute or so left me standing at the entrance of the main salon which occupies the entire ground floor. That magnificent room has many mirrors, as you'd expect in a brothel, and shaded lights, satin drapes, and carpets which suggest the Orient, but are not, alas, the real thing. Nothing, in fact, is real, which gives La Laterne the atmosphere of illusion.

When I say Marie-Claire told *me* that amusing story concerning goats, I am a trifle presumptuous. She was not talking to me alone, but also to others gathered around what they called 'the throne', a chair with arms standing on a raised platform, always occupied by whoever was in charge of the salon, as a rule by Madame Rose herself. The power of that woman, the way she instructs her girls as well as her customers, they all come under her spell. Colette assists. They say she has a hard face, though her mouth, lips that fall round and sensual, remind me of the way my mother peels apples, so skilfully, going round the fruit and keeping the skin in one piece so that it falls like a discarded skirt on to her plate. How can Colette be as hard as her reputation describes? She can, they say, read Madame's will and carries out her instructions to the letter. It is she who removes at least one garment from each visitor, or more if that's decreed. Stand still, she tells the police prefect as she removes his cap and undoes his belt and tunic, commits, in fact, the act of denuding. She taps the fellow's leg to make him lift it so that she can remove his shoes, and all this she does with such swiftness and precision that everyone is spellbound by her performance.

I digress. My mind runs wild today simply to keep warm, inspired by Annie's walkabout on the Parisian moonscape. I'll make some tea, if only to warm my hands on the hot mug, then come back to Marie-Claire's goats.

Her eyebrows are like the circumflexes Picasso has painted in his portraits of her, she has that oriental look. Nobody quite knows why she comes to La Laterne. I've tried to find out but I'm told not to ask questions like that. Like Madame Rose herself, Marie-Claire is not available *pour les clients* - for upstairs, that is. She sits there in good clothes and shows much of her beautiful legs. Her being there once, at most twice a week when she visits Paris, the cool ex-mistress of *le grand maître*, lends respectability to the illusions men crave for in the outside world and lessens their inhibitions in this house of pleasure. It's a clever and sophisticated trick of Madame's to use her old friend in this way, and a handful of her clients come specially on days when Marie-Claire is there. Most, though, walk away when she starts talking in her sombre voice, and I admire her for taking no notice of any disregard. She'd carry on even if no one were listening to her, as if she herself simply needed to give voice to some inner experience she could not describe elsewhere. That's, I believe, why she comes, for reasons not dissimilar to those of Madame's visitors, to satisfy herself. After listening to her goat story one afternoon I felt I had the right to claim some kinship with her on account of my escapade with Lothar.

'A year or so before I met Pablo,' she told us, 'I had begun to note down dreams that seemed extraordinary. Just before we met I dreamed one night that I was taking a bus trip, the sort of thing organized to show tourists famous monuments. We stopped at a museum and when we got out they herded us into a goat-shed. It was dark inside but I could see there were no goats. I was beginning to wonder why they'd brought us there when I saw, in the middle of the shed, a baby carriage. In it, and hanging from it, were two paintings. A portrait by Ingres, and a small painting by Le Douanier. Both were smaller than their actual size. The Ingres was dangling from the handle of the little carriage, the Rousseau nestling inside it.'

I noticed that whilst Marie-Claire was speaking no one moved. The half-dozen or so guests who were sitting about in their various states of undress were hooked on her voice, she kissed the air with it, such was the charm with which she modulated each sentence, as if, as indeed was the case, her experience once told now belonged to us all, as though she had lived it for us.

'A few months after I met him I showed Pablo my notebook and he then told me the Douanier in my dream belonged to him. Later on, when I had my first child, the nurse attending me was called Ingres and the midwife Rousseau. What, Pablo asked our friend Lacan at the time, is the meaning of a goat-shed? The symbol of birth, he was told.'

Marie-Claire's talks are interludes beset with decorum, a bonus on some aspect of art before the delightful skirmishes upstairs. That afternoon, however, things got a bit out of hand. No sooner had Marie-Claire told her tale than Maître Ziquet, stroking his white goatee, clambered about on his hands and knees. With each movement he grunted as if he were swallowing a lot of air, and when he reached her stockinged legs he touched her with his lowered head, then raised himself a little and licked her thighs. It was not, of course, up to us to stop him, but someone must have gone to tell Madame, for she appeared at once and prodded the illustrious advocate's backside with her pointed shoe, hard enough to make him topple over and land on his back. He shook for a minute or so like those goats Lothar had shot, and then, gathering himself up, addressed a few words to Marie-Claire, telling her that he'd meant no disrespect by his performance. 'Ziquet, my name, means little goat in the Midi where I come from. Perhaps you did not know?' Marie-Claire smiled, then brushed her stockings with her hand, and got up to leave. She walks with such grace and panache, such female elegance, you miss her the moment she's gone.

I'd like to wear Marie-Claire's clothes and assume her position on the throne and tell Claudine and Flora, and another three or four of the girls at La Laterne, about Kramer's goats. I want Colette to dress me, simply without ado or questions to put me into Marie-Claire's clothes, having warned me before-hand not to disobey her command. How could I? I am under her spell, too inert to resist, the male in me undergoing every transformation I know of into female, embracing her. There. That's as far as I can reach, *das ewig weibliche zieht uns hinan*, I can't change more than that, Maman. I'll wear for an hour your corsets and deck myself in silk and bangles, and allow you to paint my face. What pollution did you pour into my ear to poison my severance from you so that you stand like a magnet in my life which attracts every cruelty I can think of? Is that what you did with your umbrellas, use them as funnels to pour poison into my ears?

About Kramer's goats, I'd tell them how the herd is dying. All those goats can do now is to rub their udders against each other, or browse in celibate decline. I told them about the bucks Lothar had shot, and there were gasps in the audience. Oh, how terrible, how sad, those poor goats! I assume they were pining for the females of the breed.

I went on for some time declaiming from the throne, telling my listeners snippets of my life with Pablo, I was familiar with most of it. Once or twice the silk cape with the Catalan pattern slipped off my shoulders and I pulled it back. There was lots of red in the pattern, and ultramarine, red thick black lines encasing each colour, like stained glass, and I started to feed the host to my flock – oh, they all came up to me and opened their pretty mouths, and as I placed the dipped wafer I touched every one of their sweet tongues. No doubt my gestures were clumsy. I'd not, after all, had much practice in these ministrations, but I noticed from the expression on their faces as they went back to their seats, the organ piping soft legato, that as they chewed they were trying to find the taste of the spirit. I could say more of what happened but think it right not to disturb every mystery.

My money has arrived. Sabatine was kind enough to shove Maman's letter under our door. I made sure the cheque was inside, went to the bank and then the first thing I bought was coal, a fifty-pound bag I carried on my shoulder. What a welcome for Annie when she returns, a roaring fire! My mother's letter reeks of perfume, she dabs it on on purpose to carry her odour from Jo'burg to France. I'm not averse to reading her letters in winter, for I feel sure she won't announce a visit whilst it's summer in Africa. It's the reverse I dread. I like it when she tells me she's hard up, that everyone is fleecing her, the servants even have asked for more money, everything costs so much more as each month goes by. I hope she'll curtail her travels, at least cut Europe out next year so that I won't have to relate to her as I do when she comes, which breaks my distance from her. The word 'confusion' has seeped into her limited vocabulary; everything is confusion she writes several times – oh, what a confusion. It puts the lid on her half-baked ideas, shows that that satiated reptile is too lazy even to wriggle a thought to conclusion until anger makes her hungry once more, which makes her lash out with her forked tongue. I know that beast, here it comes. 'Can't you help me by finding a job? Are you not well enough yet?' She might as well ask why I'm not playing football for St Etienne or Liverpool! I couldn't, Mummy darling, stand the shock of losing. I'd not accept any decision against us by the referee and I'd walk off. I suspect the trade winds from Paraguay haven't carried any yodels from Jo for a while, hence that depressed tone of her letter. What a confusion!

Eight

I've once more come out of the madhouse. If I had enough money I'd never have to go inside again. I'd confine myself, when the time comes, to my rooms and get a medic to sedate me until the storm abates in my head. You know what it's like in a storm, when a ship is but a tossed shuttlecock to the blast and the needle in the compass, at intervals, goes round and round. It's when the storm passes that terror begins, when you're in the no man's land of consciousness before you feel once more that you are a man apart. Beware. Beware of the wet sheet they wrap round you, co-operate they say, now be a good boy. They're asking you to give a helping hand whilst they prepare for your execution. Afterwards, the shock leaves you with a splitting headache and no memory, and a few other side-effects, but it's all for your own good, my dear. They'll not catch me again. There's no point in being violent at Beaujon, since they'd overpower you and tie you up. No. I reasoned with Madame Philipponat, I actually won the doctor over with sweet reasonableness and she wondered for a moment why I was there at all, then decided to treat me only with pills and promised never to shock me again. I don't, though, trust her. I don't trust anyone.

I think that my bouts of sickness are caused by my craving for recovery. It's as if I have to be weakened in order to regain my strength, it's no more than doing with my mind what my body does every day. I love to weaken and to recover.

Today I have woken with Colette. Oh, I can spirit Annie away, with one stroke she's gone. I'll make her ill. She came back one afternoon during the cold spell, shivering all over. I told her to take a hot bath but Da Silva, she said, was entertaining one of his addicts and his bathroom couldn't be used. I made some hot tea, but her hands were shaking so much that the hot liquid spilled on her chin when she held the mug to her mouth, and she was livid like a child being forced to eat an unwanted spoonful of food, and accused me of trying to scald her. The fever went to over forty and now she's gone south to stay with an aunt at Beaulieu. She'll be out of sight for a week. I wish it were as easy as that, that I could extricate my longings at a stroke, and pursue Colette and her ilk. That is, of course, what I must do before long, before I go into that chamber of darkness where I shan't be able to see anyone or where no one will see me.

Colette asks no questions and will never leave me. The two of us are inextricably bound together, body and soul. It's as if she's been put together by magic, from past memories and odd sights and things I don't even remember because they slipped straight into my unconscious, Herr Jung, before I could record the rustle of her skirt. There's no doubt I'm in her power, she ties me to the rack, I'm an animal with little power to change my direction. When my mind goes berserk I never fail to see a sobering flash of my own insignificance, but it's always too late by then to escape the storm which I have to ride out like one of Ahab's mates.

She gets up first and I watch her dress the far side of the room. She'll undress every night like a superb stripper, in front of me, but when she puts her clothes on in the morning she doesn't want me near her. I watch her hold the mirror to her face but keep my eyes half-closed so that she won't know I'm watching her. When she comes up to the bed to prod my chin gently and stroke my cheek, I pretend to be asleep. Such games we play and never break the rules. I'm dressed in a trice and scamper downstairs to get some croissants whilst she makes the most delicious coffee. I can small it when I come back upstairs. Ours is the best-smelling room in the house. She's made the bed and stoked the fire. The room is warming up for me to work after breakfast. We report sensations to each other, physical things, things that at times are cloaked in cursory discussions of other matters. Every day I tell her the weather report I've learned from Sabatine. She's good on weather, we take directions from her and this afternoon we'll meet in the Luxembourg to see a bit of green and sit in the sun. What she does until three o'clock I won't get to know until later on in the week, or month, maybe never at all. A new scarf will one day appear on her head, or a bangle on her wrist. They blaze into life the moment she puts them on. Three weeks ago I wound some wool for her. Actually she doesn't like me to touch her things, though she's never uttered an angry word when I have done so. I had some phoning to do that day and couldn't settle down to work, as I was expecting my brother on a visit. I wound the wool over my fingers, then slid them out after a few turns. I did that to keep the yarn loose and not to stretch the texture, and she praised me and called me 'clever boy'. She knitted a cable-stitch sweater for me, the one I'm wearing today. It's soft and firm like her skin. I like what she does for me.

My mother can talk. Imagine her queening it over Colette, scoring on her position in society, embellishing her antecedents - oh, we had horses and a groom in Poland when I was a child, before my parents moved to Vienna. I was the belle of our village. Lioshka, my mother's seamstress, made the most beautiful clothes for me of tulle and organdie. How confident I felt in those clothes! I remember when we arrived in Vienna, I was six at the time, I cried when I saw all the chic women in the street and smart children walking in the Prater. Their nannies made signs by twirling their parasols this way or that. I believed for years there was some parasol code which gentlemen understood, a rendezvous could be arranged simply by a twist of your umbrella. Or: my husband, my late husband, that is, or was, if you like, I've never quite mastered the language but you know what I mean - words, I've always thought, are not as important as touch, don't you agree? - what a charmer he was, with that thick dark hair and a complexion you'd simply call dramatic. Dark eyes, brown, almost black, the sort they call full of fire, and that gentle mouth, he used to love me all over, and in between he whispered endearments which travelled up my skin and gave me the sensation of floating, and indeed we became a boat, fore and aft, and sailed into the night! I said let's wait a little longer, we were still so young, don't let's encumber our freedom with a babbling appendage, another year or two is not too much to ask for. A few harsh words that year were enough to allow him to double-cross my womb, and the twins came between us. Ah, the beauty of life – where one happiness ends, another begins! But my husband, let me tell you, he drifted away, the whispers of love grew fainter, his moods blacker, and no matter what signs I made with my beautiful umbrellas, our code was broken and he no longer read me.

Colette stands aghast listening to that yodelling prankster. Maman would like to hold a drink in her hand, she's brought some duty-free liquor and Colette fetches glasses to pour. Maman always needs to hold something in her hand to steady her nerves, particularly when faced with younger women. You can see how uneasy she feels, even I can tell, let alone Colette, by the way she fidgets with her clothes until her hand is occupied. I used, she says, to go to hotels and cocktail bars to meet my friends. Every Thursday after the hairdresser's I went to the Métropole to show off my latest coiffure, and on Saturdays I visited the club. I entertain very little at home. There are too many widows now in my circle to make it amusing, and I'm grateful for Jo's visits. You do understand, don't you? Never mind the mischief he got up to during the war. We're dead a long time. That's one of her favourite sayings, a shot she injects into her murky thinking which enables her to put aside Mengele's indiscretions and open her legs to that Jew murderer.

Colette knows how to deal with her. Her eyes, the rarest of green, follow every one of Irma's moves, her stare is deployed so as to surround her enemy. *Encore?* she asks, holding up the bottle for Irma to see. Her white and capable fingers promise well for the liquid inside. Please. What libations she pours! Her background is slightly different from Maman's. Papa drives a taxi, used to ply Les Halles, but now works the airport runs from Orly and Charles de Gaulle. Colette rode with him most afternoons whilst her mother was busy in their small apartment 'entertaining friends'. With the scant information I have about Colette you could suspect that her mum was on the game. Who knows? I've tried several times to worm the question into our conversation, but all that Colette does is to cut off my head and smile. That's for being a worm, she says, without uttering a word, and I lose my direction.

Maman takes us to La Coupole for lunch. We'll make it a pleasant occasion with a bumper meal, but she simply cannot desist from being rude and insulting about my person. He needs fattening, she says to Colette, as if Colette were responsible for my scarecrow appearance. My hair has grown again, and my eyebrows have come on a treat. God, she should see me naked, my Belsen ribs would make her double the remittance she sends, and she actually suggests establishing a figure of credit every month at our local *épicier* so that anything extra she might give will go on food and on nothing else. She discusses this as she fingers and attacks our *oursin* from the sea platter she's ordered, as if it were still alive and resisting the grip of her whetted lips and the bite of her sharp teeth. Her mastications are revolting. She's about to start discussing in detail how to set about and arrange that credit this afternoon. How can we make sure, she asks Colette, her co-opted director at this board meeting, that Fabrice doesn't make some private deal with the grocer to get money out of him instead of food? Come on, she prods my tough Colette, give a hand, make some sound suggestion, after all you'll benefit as well if you eat with my son. We all need a square meal a day. I'm fine, I plead, we have enough to eat. As if, she looks at Colette, he knew what was enough to eat! Just look at him, he weighed more as a child than he does now.

I force the food down my throat so as not to foul up Mother's good deed of the day and to mitigate her harangue. The portions they serve are too big. She goes on and on, Colette is a threat to her waning power, for she sees she can't win her over to make her my surrogate mother and force some incest into our affair. What time, Colette suddenly asks, is our train, Fabrice? We're going to see, she invents, Carpentier, a painter friend of ours who lives near Chartres. Just for two days. A little break. It was all arranged some time ago, and Jean would be most upset if we cancelled. That put the kibosh on fixing up groceries, on Irma's entire visit. She'll be gone by the time we get back. At five, I tell Colette. Just after five. I draw a number of Carpentier's pictures for Maman. I do it so well that within minutes she thinks she has seen his work somewhere.

When I work I don't hear any noise on the stairs, footsteps, doors being shut or Sabatine's ruthless shouts at someone she's missed coming into the house. The world I'm in has its own sounds, its own temperature even. Colette's gone off to La Laterne to unbutton Monsieur, and mother is up to her usual tricks in Jo'burg. Suddenly I begin to feel cold and I start hearing the usual noises on the stairs. I get up to stoke the fire and wait for Annie. She comes home around five. There's still time for me to open her cupboard and touch some of her clothes, my favourites at least, and to open the drawer where she keeps her make-up. We'll talk and talk. She'll take off her coat and scarf, rub her hands together to wash away the cold, then kiss me and loosen her belt before she sits down. I hope she will never leave me.

81

Nine

For four months now I've been well. I've left the cloister and feel a novice in the world. I'd like to hug the driver of the Métro for swifting me through subterranean Paris, or the postman for delivering a letter from hundreds of miles away. We have bought a new chest of drawers and two more chairs for our room, and once a week we invite friends for a stew which Annie prepares the night before.

I've come a long distance from the wilderness I've lived in. The state of well-being can change overnight. I've no idea what causes such change, and all's not for the better. I feel as if all the drugs I've consumed over the years, voluntarily or enforced, have taken their toll and left my sensitivity impaired. It is said that when Blake beheld the knotted root of a tree he began to weep. I followed his example many times, burst into tears when I came across a broken bough severed by the wind, lying unshrouded on the ground. Not any more. On every walk through the Luxembourg Gardens you come across unexpected disaster akin to the footsteps of chaos, and yet my eyes stay dry. I've tested this with my fingers. Even near the rim of my eyelids there's no moisture. I'm no longer moved by botanic innocence, the flower-beds trampled on by children's feet, such cruelty performed to retrieve a ball. I've given up my mercury existence and am now tough as steel.

I've written a number of stories, none are finished, but all that's needed is a day's work on each one. It's a difficult market, particularly as I have no contacts in London or New York. About two months ago I started to feel cooped up in our attic. I've spent much time there, and this, as well as the change I was undergoing, made me want to get out of the place and work elsewhere. I have a friend at the Mazarine Library just down the road from here along the Seine, and he allowed me to work at one of their grand tables. I remember the first time I actually settled down to work. Nothing but fleeting glimpses of Proust came to my mind, and of Sainte-Beuve. Both had worked in that place and my mind strayed when I thought of where Marcel had trodden or where Sainte-Beuve had sat to write his inspired critiques. I held out for only a week in that place. I felt the walls closing in on me, the lonely search for ideas and words, there was no one to talk to or to make laugh except the occasional appearance of M. Beyle, lately returned from Civitavecchia, and Scott F. came in once or twice, pissed out of his mind. He'd come to see Da Silva for a batch of drugs, and I'd helped him upstairs. You'll be flying home, I told him, when you've sniffed Da Silva's white powder he keeps for his favourite punters. He said something about having booked a white steed and to let him know when it arrived, the arsehole. I've not seen him since. That, you know, is the batty world of an author. They see things and talk to anyone who comes along with complete disregard for social behaviour or geographical distance. They're idiots who bawl and dribble odd ideas. I simply had to get out of that world to lead a normal life.

Annie had found work in the office of Robert Jaulin, the architect. His atelier in the Marais, near the Place de Vosges, had, she told me, much glass and splendid views, a light-trap constructed on top of one of the old houses. Annie liked it there. She'd often talked about finding work to bring in some money, and our stream of consumer goods started to swell. She bought me a warm shirt with her first pay-cheque. The arrangement could have worked very well, with her going out in the morning and me staying at home to do my work, but something went wrong. My work, from the very first day she went off to work, started to dry up. A temporary block. I'd had them before, but after three or four days I was still without an idea in my head. I kept getting up and looking in the mirror to see whether some weird mutation was taking place on my face, a change parallel to that inside my head. At the same time I had a sense of well-being, exactly when I should have felt rotten and distraught, but not a bit of it. I hadn't felt better or physically stronger since I'd been in my school's football team when I was thirteen. I'd come a long way since then, covered thousands of miles to escape the bourgeois squalor of my mother's house, but she'd sent the dogs after me to spoil things for me. Lice and rats were eating my words, leaving me empty and somehow, for the first time in my life, prepared, anxious even, to find a job.

For reasons my Jungian fellow might have explained over three or four sessions, waxing on about the womb and the early days of one's life, I wanted to work underground, and a wine-cellar was my choice. I think it was pride held me back from telling Annie of my intention. She had, after all, just started her job, and was working for me as well as for herself. There was danger to the balance of our life in the prospect that, in addition to my monthly remittance, I was about to contribute further funds, giving us a prosperity we were not used to. Frightened as I was of the disturbance that lay ahead, nothing could topple my plan to find work, and I set about it by going out one morning to our local wine merchant at a time I'd seen deliveries being made by a bottler and wholesaler. I remember, whilst waiting, studying the bottles and labels on display, trying to commit as many names to memory as possible, as if I were swotting for an exam. When the truck arrived I took down the address on its side and half an hour later I arrived at the Caves Frantelle Père et Fils. There was a smell of musty wine as I looked for the office, climbing a few steps up a loading bay where men were stacking cases and returnable barrels on their vans. *Le Bureau* was a shed brighly lit, and on entering I was directed, when I asked to speak to Monsieur Frantelle, to see Madame Hélène. I note that the sentences with which I describe this scene sound old fashioned, but I can't think of any other way of doing so. (No doubt that prose style was in use when

84

Frantelle Père et Fils was established in 1908.) Not that there was much of age to discern in the place. A few maps of Burgundy vineyards, and three old photographs of bearded men, the one at the centre wing-collared. At the back was M. Frantelle's office, adjoining, I later discovered, a tasting-room for his customers to sample and spit. M. Frantelle was outside, most likely down in the cellar Mme Hélène told me, and she invited me to go and look for him. I found him astride one of the hogsheads stacked three high and resting on scantles, swinging a mallet to undo a bung. He'd seen me all right, but obviously couldn't stop what he was doing and called down to apologize whilst I watched him dip a pipette into the cask, then raise it to pour red wine into a glass. There's a beauty, he pronounced after two sips, swirling the liquid round his mouth and drawing breath before swallowing – a favour to me, no doubt, else he'd have spat out even from such a height. One of the cellarmen who'd been assisting him now clambered up the cask to mark it ready for bottling. What can I do for you, Monsieur? M. Frantelle asked after his descent, shaking my hand.

Next morning I was given a green apron and started to bin the bottles filled the previous day. The fellows down there had worked in cellars all their lives. In the morning Claude made me pass bottles, which he stacked away, and in the afternoon he allowed me to do some binning. He was teaching me, telling me not to be too cautious, glass has plenty of bounce. Skill, he said, drives caution away. Don't think that the work wasn't hard, every muscle ached. For years out of tune, I wasn't used to being on my feet all day, and when we sat down for lunch, always an elaborate affair, I drank far less than my free litre of wine. What I enjoyed above all was that I had so much time to think whilst my hands did simple work, filling bottles or pulling the lever of the corking machine. I wrote many poems in my head but afterwards remembered only that dreamlike activity and not a single line.

For two weeks I carried on like that. I used Da Silva's bath more often than before, to soak my body in hot water and then feel that glow of fatigue as I went upstairs, ready for early bed.

Annie acquiesced to my new habits without a murmur. Little changes occurred. Instead of the *ordinaire* I'd purchased twice a week I now brought bottles home from Frantelle's, and Annie and I set our taste-buds on a course of instruction. She must have been most amused during my Bacchus days to hear me discuss the taste of wine with her, argue about its nose and length of flavour, our points of reference increasing as we stayed, say, with Bordeaux for a week. St Emilion has so much more fruit than Pauillac! She agreed with most of my judgements, and induced me to purchase some *crus classés* in which these characteristics were more pronounced. So we sat there some nights downing a bottle of Beaucaillou or Las-Cases with our supper, and if I hadn't stopped this nonsense before long we'd have ended up with first growths of increasingly rarer vintage. Also my bodily functions changed. Eating two meals a day, at prescribed times, and adding wine to my diet, I became, as they say, regular. Oh, there's no doubt I felt much the better for it, and Madame Parapluie would have been pleased had she known. So, no doubt, would E. Everybody teaches their children to be regular, but I tell you it knocks the shit out of you, it does exactly what that ghastly expression implies: it kills. That very support towards well-being they teach us, dragooning our metabolism, destroys. Who teaches you to laugh, or to make love at regular times? I don't want to discuss that stinking subject at length, but I tell you that regular functions, including employment, do not agree with me. I detest having my existence pushed towards that of a clerk. Thank God I found out in time, before those nurses in my head took charge of me and succoured my wounds until I had grown new skin, for I felt numb after some weeks, with anger rising which even the kindness of M. Frantelle could not still.

Two weeks after I'd started he called me to his office and asked whether I'd like to assist for a time, as part of my general training, in the order office. There'd been a rush of orders for Easter and two of his clerks were sick. I suspected that my workmates had petitioned M. Frantelle to take me out of the cellar. They could tell I'd never be one of them, that my skin would stay white, whiter even than when I'd first started, the blanching effect of working underground. I'd never drink enough wine to redden my skin, and I'd always stand out amongst them like some wretched Jonah, a good enough reason for them to throw me overboard.

Business had never been as good in the history of the firm. Deliveries were going out all over Paris, the restaurants were screaming for our wines, and with good reason. Those who'd screamed the loudest when they'd placed their orders with me over the telephone screamed louder still when they received the wrong wine the next day, and the chaos that ensued at Frantelle Père et Fils was such that my position was no longer tenable. M. Frantelle gave me my marching orders in language so foul, and I was, quite frankly, on his side for using it, that Mme Hélène sprang to my defence, telling Monsieur that no matter what I'd done, it was, after all, his fault for putting me in a position where I could cause such chaos, and she told her chief that his language was not fit for her ears, and certainly did not befit someone in his position. But M. Frantelle, at the end of his tether, was deaf to her protests and raged and railed at me until I was out of sight. Even then I doubt whether he stopped.

Why, you may ask, hit this man who was kindness itself, who gave you a job when you yourself had asked for one? Why didn't you just leave, simply not turn up for work any more and call it a day? I am ashamed, but I tell you now that I'll behave the same in the future, if not worse. It has to do with disdain, with pride and scorn, a whole thesaurus of unpleasant qualities. It emanates from some defect in my brain, a note in my octave does not ring the right sound. I don't know what it is, but I tell you whenever the time comes for the horses to run wild inside me I'm there like an idiot witness and either laugh or cry when they cavort, it makes no difference to me which it is.

I notice that my expulsion from the wine trade has not had a good effect on Annie. When I told her what had occurred at Frantelle's, laughing at my prank, describing it in detail, she joined me in part of my hilarity, but not by any means in all of it. Her refusal to do so, though she'd never objected to my behaviour in the past, jarred on me, made some of my laughter ring hollow, and made me look a fool. If that's what she had intended, she certainly succeeded. As I went on, however, trying to tear to shreds her hangups on decent behaviour with my recklessness, I could see her getting angry. She was trying to ward off my flaying of the gangster Frantelle by calling him *pauvre homme* and other endearing terms, and the word monster, monstrous at least, was at the tip of her tongue, though she was too afraid to let it slip out. Above all, though, she read my behaviour as an attack against her bourgeois world, and that's what annoyed her so. And I told her exactly that. She knew what I meant all right. Mummy's Trocadéro arms unfolding to embrace her lost daughter, the *capitaine* flaunting his cheque-book for a jaunt to Yves St Laurent. Money can buy lots of things but not your sanity, I screamed at her. I wanted her to tell me to shut up, and to take me into her arms and to tell me she was on my side.

*   *   *

I am breaking my silence. Why, I have been thinking, not be fair to yourself as well as to your brother? If you can contribute, then do. If not, shut up. I have decided a few dimensions I can fill will do no harm.

I am fond of Annie, my brother's girl. I liked her from the time I met her at Frau Eppstein's boarding-house a few days after Fabrice had arrived. I like the way she holds herself, her body straight as a die and her head held high, leaning back a little when she talks. There is character there. Fabrice was charmed by her, and quite unaware of his own beauty. I had noticed that day when I visited them that Fabrice had moved his typewriter and his papers, always the main feature of any room he lived in, from the table at the centre to a smaller one by the window. He had been out that morning to buy a fishing-rod and a jar of worms. He wanted to show them to me, and unscrewed the jar near Annie's head to make her cry out on account of her squeamishness. Annie was cutting bread for sandwiches and was pouring tea into a thermos flask, another new purchase Fabrice had made that day. We're going night fishing on Hampstead Heath, he said. I watched Annie cut the loaf. She has beautiful hands, long, elegant fingers which look capable. I like her hands very much. I also liked that air about her of untouchability, a lack of flirtatiousness that spelled an intimacy with Fabrice which had obviously been established over the few days they had known each other, and which was touching to see. God, I thought, does she know what he's like when he goes off his head? But there is also a touch of devilry about Annie. She wants to be amused, I thought, and was not averse to some rebelliousness. Fabrice had found an admirable companion to join him in his tricks.

It is not my business to comment on this now, but I can say that for the next eighteen months or so Annie had a great deal to cope with. I can read, she once told me, every light on *mon cher* pin-ball machine. That's what she called Fabrice at times, aptly I thought. When the time is up all the lights go out, and every game you play gives a different score. There is much between them. Fabrice is a fountain of magic for her where she quenches her thirst. They are like children together playing at being grown up. Oh, she knows, as he demands so often, that she must always forgive him his tantrums and bad temper and attribute their cause to some mysterious force in his make-up.

On one of my visits to Alban he asked me about Annie and I described her in as much detail as I could. Heidi was in the room at the time, that woman was always afraid she would miss something and wouldn't leave her husband alone with anyone. She listened avidly and groaned with envy whenever I mentioned France or Paris, two places the height of envy for her, for nobody, she said, looks as smart and chic as a French woman. Trust Fabrice, she said, to have landed a Parisian. Fabrice had told Alban he was going to marry Annie. I had not heard this mentioned and knew at once that Fabrice might have said this simply to inflame the skin of Heidi's envious nature, and thus I neither affirmed nor denied the rumour.

Alban gave the impression that at some time of his life he let go of ambition, like a released prisoner who couldn't overcome the shock of his sentence. I must say, in all fairness, that I always found Alban most polite and helpful. He would find out the times of trains and the opening hours of museums, obtain tickets for the opera, any such service he was only too keen to render. He kept abreast of what went on in Vienna and sent cuttings from local newspapers of matters he thought were of interest to Fabrice. This was something, in fact, Fabrice complained about. Tell that stupid cousin of ours when next you see him that I want nothing to do with Vienna, I've long lost my connections. I never had the heart to pass on the message and from time to time letters kept arriving stuffed with useless clippings. It was a reaching out for family, that's why Alban did it, somehow to keep a connection alive which had had such a shattering since his father's death and his mother's unsavoury relation. He was hurt because Maman wouldn't have anything to do with him. She believed Fabrice when he told her he had seen Alban in that dreaded uniform the year of the Anschluss, and from that day on Alban and his mother were dead for her.

Maman was about Annie's height, half a foot shorter, say. She didn't look at all like us; in fact the dissimilarity of our features was quite astonishing. Nothing, but nothing, looked related. I refer to our eyes, our chin and nose, our hands. And yet the moment she started talking you could hear the sounds Fabrice makes, the manner of his speech in spite of Maman's Viennese accent and the different timbre of her voice. She always appeared calm and was a woman of undoubted strength. The front she gave out was one of family strength, of a nature closely linked to her sons. She was most concerned with Fabrice, she knew he had not been well. She was as clever as hell at establishing a bridgehead with Annie, not in order to invade or spoil her son's intimate relations, she was far too subtle for that, but to give him background so that Annie wouldn't feel she was all alone when Fabrice needed help again. She started spinning her web within minutes of her arrival, and stayed at the centre of things until she left. Tomorrow we would do that, and we did, bought new clothes for Fabrice, added to his cutlery, replaced a leaking kettle. All kinds of repairs would be carried out whilst she was visiting. By the time she left she would have enticed Annie into accompanying her to buy clothes for herself, and reward Annie with a new skirt and a pair of saucy earrings, because, she would tell everyone, a girl with pierced ears can't possibly resist a new pair of earrings. Her own ears weren't pierced, she was always afraid to have those holes put into her ear-lobes and that, she said, was why she had so many umbrellas, thirty or forty at least, she admitted, something to dangle from her hand instead of from her ears.

Fabrice, during her visits, made her pay through the nose. He hid some of his clothes, he has made me take them to my place during her stay because she would go through his things, and was so disgusted at what she found that she would take him on a shopping spree, when she would also buy a thing or two for me, shirts and expensive sweaters I could ill afford. Within minutes of seeing Fabrice she would take him aside as she did with us in the old days when visitors came and our hair wasn't brushed or our nails weren't up to standard, and tell him to go and use the nail-file, and your teeth are really in an awful state, didn't you use the extra money I sent for the dentist? she asked him. He laughed and told her in a loud voice, so that everyone would hear, that his teeth were fine, they were as tough as steel, he boasted, and looked for something hard to bite on, and the reason they were slightly discoloured was because we had had stewed cherries for breakfast. *Les cerises noires* are something the French are so fond of, he said, sidling up to Annie. It gives Frogs that marvellous shiny complexion, didn't you know? It was charming the way he clowned about in front of Maman to make her laugh. She laughed all right, she had not forgotten how to. But she didn't thank her lucky stars when she found Fabrice so healthy and jolly that time she first met Annie. She kept on complaining about his neglected yellow teeth, his lack of weight, she would talk to him later about those horrible pricks on his forearm, those sores he couldn't keep on hiding by pulling his sleeve down because they reached too far down towards his hand. To accept his well-being would show that she was out of touch, and she certainly wasn't that. She had been around many times when Fabrice had slipped into hell, and waited for him to emerge sore and subdued like a scalded kitten, and was there all right to lick his wounds.

Every time she came to England she thanked me for all I had done, as if I were my brother's keeper. It was not a compliment I liked. She was always attempting to get me on her side and failed to understand that the ties I had to my twin brother were closer than mine to her. It was hard for me to express my feelings of inquietude when she started on that tug of war she was always bound to lose.

What about Dr Menges, our family doctor, your friend, with whom you were indiscreet all our life? There were so many peep-shows, did you know, when we were the height of your bedroom door keyhole, that filled our eyes with surprise and our heads with bewilderment. That's how Fabrice found a niche for Mengele, that Jew murderer. When the railing in his mind gets going he sees you've taken off your shoes whilst entertaining the doctor on one of his visits, and they've tumbled over at the side of your chair. And a bit later, through that keyhole, he sees you've discarded your clothes and the doctor is doing as he's told and follows you to bed. Do you remember that time when we were seated at table and Papa started to shout, when he banged the carving knife on the table-top and the steel knot of the handle seared the wood? Remember that? Was Dr Menges the cause of Papa's anger or was it, as Fabrice would put it, some other yodelling fool? When we were sick Dr Menges came to see us, and we used to be frightened in case he decided not to make us well again because of your manipulations behind closed curtains. Fabrice once called you a fucking funeral director!

Annie stayed aloof from Maman. She had not bargained to be part of the family and drew a distinct line she would not allow Irma to cross. For once Fabrice had a foot in both camps, but he

92

was cunning enough not to overplay his hand in case the two women should gang up against him. He was always at his sweetest the last day of Maman's visits, and made promises we all knew he wouldn't keep. By this time Irma too was in a good mood. It appears there were always these awkward signs one could so easily misread, that she would be glad to get away, she was longing for a few days in the Austrian Alps, a left-over joy of her youth, or the tender warmth of Nice. She was pleased with what she had accomplished in London, she had done her duty by her sons and seen several business gents in the city. Done any arms deals, Mum? Fabrice quipped some evenings when she returned for supper, but she wouldn't let on where she had been, or what business she had been up to. Something to do with import-export, she said. She was never more explicit than that. What was touching to see during those last days were the frills she had bought, the shops in London are so *vornehm*, so very elegant. Her accent became more pronounced the longer she stayed. She showed some of her purchases to us all, yes, yet another umbrella, I simply couldn't resist the sweet little thing, and scarves and bangles. Other items she showed only to Annie, lipsticks and lingerie, the latest eye-shadow for her beautiful eyes, and other titbits of lotions and sparkles for her person. You could see her walk off with her bag of tricks, preparing herself in some hotel bedroom for the bar downstairs, the adventuress. She prodded your ribs with her restlessness, and we were all glad when she had gone. Though she didn't go completely for some time, for Fabrice took over and for several days he ruthlessly mimicked her. He copied her accent to a T and cavorted about the room swinging his arms, pulled up his trouser-leg to show his laddered stockings, and talked about the little missiles he'd bought in the city which he'd sell to the highest bidder, black or white. He assumed her person with consummate and frightening skill and he could keep up his act without a break all day long, there was no intermission during the performance. It was an uncanny thing he did every time she left, an exorcism. I am sure that when he peed during that time, he sat on the lavatory. It was amusing to watch his mimicry, though he did go on for too long. Annie joined in his game. She either laughed with him or they had serious conversations. He even got her to talk about Fabrice - oh, for God's sake be careful, I felt, when I was there at the time, or she'll tell you things you may not want to hear.

Ten

Book Three starts here.

* * *

I read danger when I can't fill my vacancy. Suddenly my head is empty, my chest hollow, my legs feel as if someone has cut my calf muscles. Hold on, else you'll float away, some force will suck you through the window and the wind will smash you against the nearest chimney-pot and break your skull. We need the brotherhood of man, to belong, to see how others live, because we haven't the strength always to be pioneers in a new world, fording rivers and setting up new outposts. There are times when I simply don't know where to go, or how Sabatine, after a bad bout of flu, can ever recover her strength, and what for? I see that miserable janitor in her draughty cage and can't think what she's thinking about, what can possibly keep her going for another hour. Then I stumble upon it, it's always the same: physical sensation and nothing else saves us. Sabatine looks forward to her *pot-au-feu*, and her *compote de Mirabelle* spiced with vanilla to bring out the flavour of the yellow fruit. I get up to munch a biscuit. For a minute or so I'm occupied with crunching, and my dead mouth is enlivened by flavour. That's how we carry on, no better than animals except, by and large, we make less noise and don't shit all over the place. I know that work fulfils, and that ambition drives people to certain joys,

95

and that there are honourable spin-offs like art which festoon our existence. But I'm on about the interstices, those gaps between. At times I cannot eat enough to fill them, or find words to stuff those holes.

I've lately found a new companion, not a prince exactly, but a creature nevertheless who's lain under a spell inside me for many years. I used to have him about the house, set him under the table or put him in my mother's bed. He was really alive and Louise paid heed to him, my mother too. I think that was when I first started to frighten them all, with my dybbuk companion. He actually started his life as a radiator cap on my father's red Ford. I remember just being able to reach Bonzo by stretching myself to full height and getting hold of his iron head and pulling myself up on the bumpers. That way I could see him close by, his mainly dog, part lion and owl's features, a silver creature with black grooves. Whenever Papa put water in the radiator he allowed me to hold Bonzo. He was always warm. When the car was sold Bonzo moved in with me and we became inseparable companions. Sometimes I carried him around, but that often proved cumbersome because of his weight. Most of the time, therefore, he lived on the shelf by my bed, above and behind my head, a place he'd not move away from all day. I knew he'd be there when I went to bed at night, and I also knew he was there when I needed him during the day. Perhaps you think that all this is daft, but let me tell you you can't find anything more reliable than an idol. And Bonzo was that for me, and more. Children are never given enough attention. Grown-ups have long forgotten how to relate to them. They teach them a few rudimentary things, to keep clean and to confine their smells to the toilet, but they don't ever inform you of what your back is like, square centimetre by square centimetre, to enable you to become so familiar with your back that you really feel it is part of you. The fact that I've never seen my back without the aid of a mirror has a haunting quality about it. It disturbs me so much that at times I really don't know whether I exist at all. I remember sitting down at my table one day when Bonzo asked me if I knew whether the paper in front of me wanted to have a picture painted on it. It did. I was into drawing horses at the time and, having done the head, I wondered whether the horse wanted to be painted. Bonzo, of course, had inspired that question, and ever since I've looked at paintings that way, asking those same questions. You can tell when there are not only magic brush-strokes, but also the magic which inspired those questions. I've known myself to be angry with Bonzo when all kinds of things have gone wrong in my life, and I've taken hold of him and dropped him on the balcony floor, a nice concrete surface, to make him suffer a scratch or two. On the whole, though, he overcomes his ordeals with far less damage than I do. He's really tough, as idols should be, and I don't really know what kind of holocaust it would take to melt him away.

I've not, let me tell you, brought Bonzo to Europe with me. When I came away I left him standing on the shelf by my bed. Nobody in that Jo'burg household would be foolish enough to throw him out. I'd know all right, it's one of the connections I keep up all the time, and in the same way as I know, I'd bring a curse on that house which would cripple the people who live there. So Louise, that sorcerer's apprentice, wouldn't dare tamper with Bonzo, nor would that witch whose power I'd drain at the drop of an umbrella. I need him whenever I seek approval. How often, when I look at Annie, when I watch her move by our little sink or see her rise on her feet and see her levitate inside me as she arouses my desires with her sweetness, have I addressed myself to Bonzo. Look, I say, at that sweet woman, look at what is happening to me, and he nods his approval and I get up to embrace her from behind, and she turns her head in that marvellous embrace so that I can kiss her. Or when I make her laugh her eyelids become Japanese fans which open as her eyes almost shut. Look how she laughs! I need someone to show off my joy, to share my overspill. Or to disapprove when I let go of myself, when I sink into dejection and lose control, when I curse my engine and make it malfunction until it stalls altogether. At times Bonzo is my last resort who helps me crawl out of the pit. What have I done, just you look at yourself, where has it all gone wrong? Whenever I can, I retrace my steps and start again. And something else he does, my little Bonzochen. He makes no demands on me. I've not to provide for him in any way, not from one year to the next. No money, no food or drink, no polishing even. This kind of self-sufficiency I respect enormously. He has an inner life which hardly touches mine, as if I gave him a juicy bone for his lunch every day.

Having been born, as it were, on a car radiator to which he was screwed, Bonzo sits permanently in a squatting position. You have no idea how that position befits him, but I'll give you one. The way he squats helps me ward off disdain and haughtiness, my pet aversions. I don't know why it is, but when I come across insolent condescension I feel slighted to the quick. My supra-renals start playing up, the adrenalin flows. At that moment I'm ready to kill, but as I pick up the hammer or the carving knife, old squatting Bonzo beckons me to desist from pursuing my victims, and instead to view them squatting on the toilet with their pants down. He calms me down, my pet, and puts my anger to rest.

Apropos of anger, here's what happened three months ago after my career in the wine trade. Before my adventure at Frantelle's Annie used to return from work at five thirty-five. If she was ten minutes late the first thing she'd do would be to explain what had delayed her, the purchase of a lettuce or some other trifling diversion on her way home. Annie has never been a great talker, but being French she nevertheless talks far more than I do and uses the daily events of her life as material. We all do, I know, but she was inclined to give a full account of her day, at times with delightful asides, trills of a Bach fugue. A woman she'd seen at a shop-window, what she'd worn, the colour of her stockings, and the way she'd held a gloved finger to her cheek so that you could almost hear her debate with herself whether or not to go and try on that dress she'd been looking at. Quite often she comes out with such charming observations.

It wasn't for three days after I stayed home once more that I noticed Annie came back an hour later than before, and when I asked her the reason she pretended at first not to hear, and then looped an excuse together like a fallen stitch she was gathering back to knit into a lie. The architect was keeping her late. M. Jaulin was working on two sites at present, she had to accompany him every afternoon and take down notes for him. Plausible. Very. But note she was out of the office every afternoon, so when I started to become suspicious I couldn't easily check up on her. If I did and she found out there'd be hell to pay, not that I'd mind when it came to it. But I didn't stand in good odour with Jaulin. I'd once, over the phone, cracked a bad joke, and called him a jerry-builder. I remember when I used that expression I felt I'd overstepped the mark of propriety and hoped to God he didn't know what it meant. But he did and he gave me quite an earful and Annie told me he'd called me *un idiot*, an epithet she didn't enjoy when applied to me. Most of the time I didn't believe in these afternoon jaunts of Annie's with her architect, they didn't ring true. There was no shred of evidence on her person, a slither of mud on her shoes, though she did go in for low heels and even flat shoes at the time. When she came home I used to sniff her like a dog. I did it playfully, leaped at her and laid my head on her chest with my tongue out. *Ne me moleste pas, chéri*, she used to cry out when she had something delicate or fragile in her bag, it was a pot of flowers once, but usually eggs for our supper. But my sniffing, though fun, was no idle cavort. I wanted to find out where she'd been. I sniffed for cement and lime, or another man's smell. Sometimes I thought I'd caught some suspicious odour, but I was always left perplexed. I once asked her where the sites were she was visiting. Fifteen kilometres apart, on the outskirts of Paris. The more plausible her lies, the more my suspicions were aroused, which in turn made me suffer the swings of that terrible pendulum, doubt. I didn't go through her things. Every day I spent at least an hour, wasted an hour of my life, debating with myself whether or not I should go to that secret drawer where she kept private mementoes. Several times she'd shown me everything inside that drawer and told me the stories attached to each object. Was there anything new, an unfamiliar note, a

button or the tassel of a scarf? But I always desisted –
sometimes, when my fingers were itching to open the drawer,
almost too late. It was too risky to disturb the skin of our love,
it could so easily be pricked, never to heal again. Make no
mistake, I went through hell that month and she played her role
so well that I suspected her all the more. And that exacerbated
my anger, for at the best of times I suspect women of playing
roles. It's the way they dress up, the planning of beauty, the way
they add to themselves, to play their hypnotic act. Come, my
dear, I know I've got your heart started, now do the rest! It's
their command to enchantment.

For a whole month I didn't ring Annie's office or visit the
sites to check up on her story. I was all the time engaged in my
suspicions of her, terrified of a break-up, and did hardly any
work. I got stuck with a poem and had to abandon it. The force
of the first four lines didn't carry me through to the fifth. You
may say that the force was too weak, but that's not so. After the
first gush of words I need tranquillity, and there was none that
month. Nothing came to my mind except a few notes I wrote
about my turbulence, which I'm using to write this down.
Here's one: his biscuit complexion and a crossed loaf for a kiss.
Who's eating her? Another: she's inside me ever since that
sweet bacillus entered me, spreading like a disease.

Half-way through the month I started to feel quite numb,
like after heavy sleep, I recall. All the features of my face feel
stiff, my mind too. I can't continue where I left off yesterday, a
link seems to be missing. Until I throw off that sluggishness I
stay numb, and even when I'm once more fully awake I feel
nothing will be the same again. Don't think I'm not unaware
that better things may happen than before, but I'm at risk.
Annie was different, some change had taken place. Her skin, I
heard a whisper of writhing when I touched her, there was an
added shyness when she dressed, I caught vacant looks I'd not
seen before, her handbag which she'd sort out once a week,
emptying everything on the table in front of me, she kept shut.
Yet she was so kind that month and sweet, that when Bonzo
suggested I should see her with her pants down I told him to get

stuffed and totally rejected his advice. And then one day she came home radiant, saying she'd passed, clutching a driving licence in her hand. That's where she'd been those extra hours, learning how to drive! She'd tricked me for a whole month to fashion her surprise, and though I was happy to lay my forays of doubt to rest, the price I'd been forced to pay so she could keep her secret was too high.

I need some distance from myself, a short breathing-space, and so will try writing in the third person.

Annie rented a car and asked Fabrice to come away with her for the weekend. They left late morning and by the time they reached the outskirts of Paris Fabrice felt relaxed with his new driver. *Le capitaine* had given Annie fifty thousand francs for passing her test, a gesture he'd made without too much prodding from his wife. He was fond enough of his daughter, but she was living with a man with no future. A little cash might drive a wedge between them, a gamble worth taking. Not that Annie fell for this trick. She immediately told Fabrice what her father had done and made her cash their common property. All, that is, but ten thousand francs. A woman needs a little in reserve.

Monsieur and Madame were driving through the French countryside. They'd decided to avoid the *autoroute* to get some country air into their lungs instead of petrol fumes. Fabrice was overcome with a contentment new to him. Annie looked attractive, she'd acquired an English hacking jacket for the occasion, a confident young housewife who, you could tell, had made the beds and cleared the sink before leaving. The point of return, after all, is so important. The day before she'd got her husband's prescription, the pills he'd been taking for some time under doctor's orders. When his temper was foul she put it down to those pills. Tough little wifie, she saw to everything and made allowances where they were due. One has to overcome life's little ups and downs, at least one of the partners has to be sensible. And the children, ah, those dear little mites, they were well looked after by Aunt Sabatine, who'd feed them and see that they went off to school on time. On Sunday Annie's parents would look after them, and they'd wheel Grandpa to the restaurant. Did you know that Annie's maman was of Italian descent? As a child of four she'd seen her father shot dead in front of their house. What a handsome fellow he'd been! Annie had some of his looks, the dark hair and sensual mouth. *A crime passionnel.* His lover's husband did him in, what a thing to do, and the young widow and the child moved in with her unmarried sisters, a jolly household in Clichy, the abode to this day of two old maiden aunts. And then Maman had married into the army, quite an obvious choice if you think of it, for a girl whose life had been affected by a bullet.

At one o'clock sharp, though they'd not driven far, they stopped by some poplars for a kerbside picnic. Nothing came to Fabrice's head as they sat uncomfortably on the ground to share a slab of pâté and some wine. Passing cars kept interrupting the silence, you could hear them buzz towards you from far away in both directions, so much so that all silence was spoiled by the expectation of the next interruption. Annie, in some detail, appraised the pâté, garnishing her opinion with the alternatives she could have bought at the *charcuterie*. She peeled an apple and gave two quarters to Fabrice, then poured some coffee from the thermos. How well she provided in the middle of a war, for that's what Fabrice was at, playing war-games. Whenever he visited the country, that's what he did. How the devil could troops move across this flat terrain, cover the next kilometre without loss? There was relief when you came to the hills, mountains were cowboy territory, a sniper's dream. He liked these primitive games, hunting and killing and escaping enemy bullets. Man is a hunter.

Late that afternoon they arrived at the Val des Cousins, through which runs that marvellous river which roars like gathering echoes. All the noise of the valley is caught in it. They could hear it through the closed windows of their room. Those who love them know that rivers have godlike qualities. If you stare at the water, try, your mind becomes dumb as those stones made smooth by centuries of submersion. The river envelops you, draws you close as one of its creatures – watch out, and catch your breath in time to keep going.

Fabrice felt uneasy in the country and slept close to Annie. In the morning after breakfast in their room they had a warm bath and used all the towels stacked out for their use, and then he watched his wife dress, putting her clothes on, sheathing her pretty body. That was nice. Still in her underwear, sitting on the bed, Annie rang her mother to inquire about the children. No, she'd rather not speak to them, it might unsettle them, she just wanted to know if they were all right. Oh, wonderful, the hotel is so comfortable, it's so nice not to have to do any housework for a few days, such a change. She lied about the pleasure it gave her, and then converted that lie into a feeling of well-being as she began actually to feel what she'd told her mother. Fabrice, let us be fair, ever since he'd settled down with a complete stranger, was a spectator of the bourgeois circus. The more he attempted to run away from family life, the more charming he became to his wife, his aloofness attracted her, though she couldn't for the life of her read in his work what he was about. How could he translate for her those inward spin-offs of the poet, as when they passed the graveyard on their drive to Vézelay and the cathedral seemed to rise like a liner on the waves of the hills, with music coming from the valley? He thought of dead musicians, drummers and cello players, their dexterity buried in their silent coffins, their grins of death an apposite expression for the miracles of sound they'd once performed on their instruments. Or of Bonzo squatting in the jungle of his mother's house, sending messages to him. He was as close to him as to his heartbeats, closer than to Annie.

Jotted down a few pages in the third person, just as I said. No reason why I shouldn't. Sometimes I want to escape, to transform and be part of that transformation. Suddenly the chase is on, it's imperative for me to get away, not only to get elsewhere but to reach a different state of existence, to become

103

someone else even. Don't hide from me the fact that sooner or later they'll come to take me away. Oh, we had a few exquisite days in the country, such quietude compared with what goes on now, though I remember those wretched mosquitoes by the river, their buzz screaming into my ears, my hands swatting the air to drive them away but for one of their infinite number which drew my blood. I'm not under arrest but don't know how much longer I shall be free. Everywhere I get caught, and I'm not surprised. It started, E., when I stopped thinking about Annie when I fucked her. I think of other things, other women, glimpses that have stuck to the membrane of memory since childhood. I noticed in my war-games there was nowhere to hide, they'd be there surrounding the copses and woods, waiting for me to emerge in order to grab hold of me. The women blindfold me and drive me back to the house of detention. I find out nothing from the effeminate conversation of the women in the limousine - how pretty those trees are shrouded in the mist, Charlotte did my hair, always does, I wouldn't let anyone else touch it. Where are we, where's that house of detention, what neck of the woods? There are high walls, high windows. Everything directs you to what's going on inside the place, and I won't tell you what it is because they've commanded me not to speak about it. If I do they'll whip me in no uncertain fashion in a room especially assigned for punishment. I am, you see, locked in.

Eleven

I'm burying Maman solo, which is just as well, because bereavement is a strictly private matter. At the time when it happened my brother was in the Alps, sojourning in a remote hut, away from it all, making arduous excursions to get fit after a year in that stuffy museum. He always spends his annual leave looking after his body, and gives his mind a rest.

Did you know Jews don't keep bodies disinterred for long? As a rule we bury the day after death, though an extra day can be tolerated, but no more. That's why there was no point in chasing Julien to come home. There simply wasn't time. In any case, I felt, one was enough to represent the two of us at Maman's funeral. I cabled them to say I was on my way back and then spoke to Louise in the evening from the airport. Master Fabrice, come home, she said through her tears. She repeated herself over and over, her plaints grew louder and longer, her sorrow, in fact, cost a fortune, but finally she understood that I was on my way. Just died, your mother, on the sofa, with her clothes on, in the middle of the afternoon.

In the first throes of bereavement I felt, I admit, privileged. Everyone focused their grief on me, Sabatine first, as I read in her presence the cable she'd brought up. She said telegrams always brought bad news, she'd known the moment it arrived it contained a message of death. I felt very awkward when she expressed her condolences, tried not to listen to those banal phrases as I prepared myself for her ultimate embrace before she went downstairs. How, I was wondering, could I avoid that moist nose touching my cheek? I made myself as tall as I could so that I was in control the moment it happened. Annie, thank God, had not yet left for work when Sabatine came up. *Pauvre garçon* she said, how very sad, you must of course go at once. She rang Jaulin from Sabatine's cage and told him she'd not be there that day, and we went to buy a shirt for me and a black tie and a ticket for Jo'burg that night. We made love in the afternoon, I remember the gentleness of it all. Parting from Annie didn't hit me until the plane was up in the air, when the captain announced his flight plan. By the time we reached thirty thousand feet I was all alone.

There was no one at the airport to meet me. I'd been away for four years and hadn't kept in touch with anyone. They searched my valise, and whilst the officer unzipped it he kept on talking to his colleagues, which slowed down his probe. His hand snaked its way through my bag, the writhing stopped once or twice when his digits hit on some object or another, and all the time his conversation with his mates took precedence over the work in hand.

'I'm in a hurry, man,' I told him.

'What's the hurry?'

'I've come for my mother's funeral.'

The officer looked at me, then screwed up his eyes and laughed. 'That's good, man. Hey, we've got a joker here!' With that he tipped up the contents of my valise. 'You travel light.' Having touched everything, he proceeded to put the stuff back in the bag. 'Have a good time in our beautiful country!'

'Thanks.'

'And watch your tongue.'

I thought it best to laugh. Anything to get away from that ponce and that custom-shed.

Louise said she'd been standing by the door for hours, waiting for me to arrive. When she heard the taxi she came to the gate, and when I turned to face her she held up her arms and burst into tears. She hugged my hand, clung to me when she made those terrible noises of sorrow, then, after a minute or so, released her grip and tapped my back with her hands. 'You ring Dr Menges. He's made all the arrangements. Came to see your dead mother and had her taken away.'

It was a hot evening and it wouldn't be cool for hours. When I entered the house the first thing I saw was the rack stuffed with Mother's umbrellas. I suddenly felt in an expansive mood, free at last of my maman's encumbrance. I went almost at once to see her clothes and to open the drawers with her underwear, the nearest I'd be in touch with her once more. I then felt a trifle sad at having lost that sparring partner of my life. Her unrecorded voice would badger me no more with admonishments, and my insults had lost their prime target. What was the good of saying that your fanny will be ravaged by worms, that death has finally hooked you to curtail once and for all your disgusting escapades, your yodelling copulations with Josef Mengele? I'd ask Louise whether he'd visited recently, whether perhaps it was he who'd given mother one final injection to send her on her way. I'd put nothing past him, nor her. But the room didn't respond to my jousting thoughts, the knight I'd fought was dead. I wondered for a moment, before going down to ring Dr Menges, whether I could arrange for the graveside to be sprayed with hoses so that we could bury Maman with umbrellas over our heads, a nice final gesture. Then I decided simply to take a brolly myself, which I'd open up the moment the ceremony began. Jews, after all, have to cover their heads, and that, I decided, would be my covering.

Naturally, on that sunny day of my mother's funeral, I looked a touch peculiar with one of her bright umbrellas. Not only that, but I started to giggle several times during the service before they wheeled her to the grave. That dreadful Menges fellow, and one or two of her cronies like Schloss, our lawyer, looked aghast at my brolly gesture, but the rabbi, his eyes half closed with emotion, either hadn't noticed or didn't care, and some of my late mother's female friends were, I thought, quite glad to find an excuse to interrupt this sad occasion with a smile, and thought my clutching one of Mother's umbrellas was quite endearing. I was thinking, if you must know, less of

107

Maman's imminent disposal than of the disposal of her personal belongings, and I giggled, couldn't help it, when I thought of myself being looked at by these women, this poor orphan with a history of disturbances, we'll have to rally round to take care of him, help him tackle his domestic problems, poor child, he can't even boil an egg. I'll show you how well I can take care of myself, you old cows. I'll make you slip inside your corsets, which will wrinkle your stockings.

The moment we got back to the house I went to my mother's room with Louise to bundle up Irma's belongings. At first Louise worked with gusto, but when she came to Maman's dresses she slowed down, and in between bursts of tears her eyes veered towards the big mirror until she couldn't resist holding one or two dresses against her to see what they looked like on her. Sure, she must have done so umpteen times before she cleared up Mother's room in the morning, and my mother had frequently handed things on to her. Not that Louise was the same shape. She was almost twice her size all round, so only loose-fitting garments could be considered. I decided, for fun, that Louise should give me a fashion parade, and although she resisted at first, she gave in with some giggling and went off to the dressing-room to put on the first dress. Put on some rouge and paint your lips, I told her when she went off for the second dress, and then she came out in Irma's vermilion gown looking quite la-di-da. My mother had some snake-skin belts which I made Louise wear, and some fox collars, complete skins with the heads intact. I made Louise put one round her neck, and got hold of that extraordinary hat with multicoloured feathers, and we cut off the wide rim to make it look more suitable on Louise. And there were boxfuls of bangles that I made Louise slide up her smooth black arms as high as she could, and at a certain point of this masquerade Louise started to hold up her arms like a TV aerial which made her hear music, for then she began to dance with fluid Negro grace. I told her to take whatever she wanted, but to remove it from the house that day, and to bundle the rest together. I then rang a charity to take the stuff away, including twenty-eight of Maman's thirty-five umbrellas.

The others I kept for their pretty handles.

Schloss, our lawyer, came with the others for evening prayers. What, E., does it mean if a man picks his nose all the time? Does Herr Jung enlighten us on this disgusting habit? That, apart from being a tough lawyer, is what Schloss was known for, picking his nose. He just couldn't leave it alone. All the years of digging had enlarged his nostrils, which were covered with coarse skin. He had a deep voice and was pleasant enough to talk to, a man with humour, but you weren't ever sure whether he'd get through a sentence before he'd start on one of his choking coughs, the result of smoking cigars.

'I've brought you this to get on with,' he said as soon as he arrived, handing me a nice clean envelope with my name on it. 'You and your brother are well provided for, very well, young man. Your mother left strict instructions.'

He almost choked on that word. Served him right, I thought. Instructions, my arse. *I* now give instructions, no one else.

'I'll drop in at eleven tomorrow to discuss matters,' I said.

He nodded his head in agreement and went on coughing. Then his voice crawled back up his ticklish throat. 'Fine,' he said. 'Eleven'll be fine.'

He spoiled things for me, that unpoetic ponce. I thought, standing there for prayers to begin, how nice of Schloss to have brought some cash, and hoped it'd be a sum greater than I'd ever handled. All my life I'd been handed sums my parents had calculated for my needs – one-sided calculations, I assure you, as I'd never been consulted. The reward for survival surely is to be master of your own affairs. When I unsealed the envelope in the loo it contained fifty rands, just enough to pay the rabbi for his unctuous song.

Next day at ten-thirty I was there. I'd got there half an hour before my appointment, hoping to find out all the sooner the amount of our inheritance. Nor was it with the best motive. I was anxious to ring Annie at Jaulin's office and boast about the amount. That, I found, was all I wanted to tell her, and one or two of the amusing details of the last two days, though it didn't, in fact, feel like two days, as I'd flown in the night. The sum was hefty all right, one hundred and eighty thousand each plus the house to split, and I laughed in spite of yesterday's funeral when the old boy came out with it.

'And there'll be more than that. But that's the sum set aside on trust for you, entirely for your benefit. I'm one of the trustees, and Frau Horngrad is the other.'

I didn't like the sound of that.

'You mean every time I want money I have to ask you for it, or that tight-arsed *corsetière*?'

'If you want to put it like that, yes. She was your mother's best friend, and you always frightened your mother with your ways. Frau Horngrad will keep you in check, and so shall I, that I promised your mother, but there'll be plenty for you to live on, and the capital will stay soundly invested. Around fifteen thousand a year you'll each get, you're rich young men.'

A few moments ago I felt so angry that I was about to tell Schloss to take all the money and stuff it up his arse. I didn't want to have anything else to do with Irma, her rule from the grave. But then I suddenly got tired, so listless I could have fallen asleep on the chair simply by closing my eyes.

'We'll keep you in funds until probate is granted,' Schloss said. 'And in the meantime you can decide what to do with the house. Where would you like to live? In Europe?'

I told him I'd no idea, which was true.

'Well, there's no hurry,' Schloss said. 'I expect you'll stay here for a while to clear things up. There's plenty of time.'

'Yeah.'

I thought I'd caught a bug I felt so worn out. All I wanted to do was to get out of that lawyer's office and go to bed, and that's what I did. I told Louise not to disturb me, and after she'd brought me some lemonade she closed the door behind her and I didn't reappear until the next morning.

Apparently they came again for evening prayers that night but had the sense not to wake me to come down. God forgives the sick and the infirm. I still felt weak when I got up, numb in the head, I couldn't get my thoughts moving, and sat the whole morning in one of the easy chairs, staring at the room and holding my head. I felt quite peaceful, no humming in the ears, if that's what you're thinking, a human instrument of perception which simply wasn't switched on. I suppose part of me was engaged in the act of acquisition; it's something like the inaudible dog whistle to the human ear, you're not aware the dog inside you stirs. You're overwhelmed by possessions you've never owned before, they suddenly clamour for attention. It makes you quite sick, in fact, the way they scream at their new owner to have repairs seen to after years of neglect. Little did they know, some of those worn chairs in the room, and several other items about the place, that if they continued to pester me with their ungainly wounds I'd throw them out and burn them in the yard.

I hadn't rung Annie since I'd got back because I felt so severed from her and didn't know whether it was wise to speak to her in that state. I know sex and death are supposed to have some connection, but confronted as I was with love a few thousand miles away and my mother's dead body fresh in the ground near by, I simply couldn't connect. That, perhaps, was the cause of my feeling of numbness. I've no idea. E., no doubt, would have several explanations at the ready, spinning out the dreary hours of analysis, his thumb up his arse to indicate death and his other hand fingering the genitalia of his patient. We were simply cut off, Annie and I. My return to Africa for family reasons had forced all those undulations of personal history to appear before us, so much so that for hours on end, for days even, I didn't think about her until suddenly there she was, so clear in my vision, like a bell tone, as if she'd just arrived fresh and chic from Paris. When I rang her that twerp Jaulin answered the phone, and I think he stood hovering behind her when she spoke, because she didn't sound as warm as I expected, didn't once ask when I'd return or should she come to Jo'burg. Neither journey, in fact, was on my mind, and I didn't tell her the amount Irma had left me. She was pleased I was well looked after, and that I was calm. Though just before saying goodbye she said she missed me, whispered it into the mouthpiece, and I felt flayed by her tenderness.

111

I felt so good after that call, I even tried walking on my hands, because suddenly everything seemed possible. Imagine my feelings when two days later first thing in the morning a pot of azaleas arrived delivered on instructions from Paris by Fest's Nursery, with a note: *With tenderest thoughts. Love Annie.* That decided me to tie up my affairs in Jo'burg at once and to return to Paris. I'd had it in mind to put the house on the market and to get rid of Louise and the houseboy. That'd be sensible, Schloss agreed, but I'd not told Louise, and I left her in charge of the place when I returned to Europe a week later.

I might as well fill in my flying time to Paris with an event which greatly disturbed me during the week before I left Jo'burg. I had called for a taxi to take me into town for one of my several visits to Schloss that week. I was sleeping badly and was glad when the light broke, the dawn being confirmed by chicken noises and the infectious barking of dogs in the neighbourhood. God knows what Louise and the houseboy were up to at this hour, but they were always about when I woke, doing some chores. I watched them one morning through the chink in the curtains repairing the washing-line across the yard with great ineptitude. It was bound to come undone the next time they hung up the washing. Perhaps, I thought, they're afraid they'll be sent away because there's nothing for them to do, so they build fragile things that need constant repairs to keep them busy. (I have hours yet on the plane and therefore have time to digress.)

I was early for my appointment with Schloss, and asked the driver to set me down at the park. I had time to walk across past the lake to the other side. The same water-birds inhabit the lake as I used to feed from my bag of bread when I was a child. I've no idea how long they live. Louise would take me there, she had her favourite amongst the Japanese ducks. Spread, their wings are floating fans. I stood by the water and remembered hurting my knees leaning against the low iron rail skirting the lake when trying to bend over to get as near to the ducks as possible. I went through my pockets trying to find something edible for them –

no doubt, E., would say, a treasure-hunt inspired by the magic finds women used to produce from their handbags, a sweet, or an indiarubber like the one I was given unexpectedly in the middle of a walk by one of my mother's acquaintances.

As I turned to walk on to keep my appointment, a man wheeling a pram let go of the handlebar and threw up his hands as he called out my name. 'Fabrice! Fabrice, man. Good God, what are you up to?' The pram had freewheeled a few yards, so the fellow had to get hold of it else he would have come over to embrace me. 'Fabrice – I'm Al Levine, remember?'

I felt obliged to say yes, though I had no idea who he was. He tried to help.

'Levine from IVb.'

He laughed and took off his hat and his horn-rimmed glasses to help me recognize him. I laughed at him and shook his outstretched hand. That, as far as he was concerned, assured him I knew who he was.

'How come you live in Jo'burg and I never see you around? Been inside or something?'

'I live in Europe.'

As I now had no time to talk in the park he asked me to come round to his house later and he gave me his address. It wasn't far from where I lived and I told him I'd be there between four and five. I spent two or three hours there with him and his wife, and though I found out exactly who he was, I still couldn't remember him. There was nothing, not one feature of his, I recognized from the past, not even when he showed me a photograph of our football team where we stood next to each other. Over and over again I looked at Levine, grilled him with my eyes, but nothing came back to me, not one tiddler could my memory catch from his person. After an hour or so I simply played games with Levine and his comely wife, made up in middle-class fashion, good clothes and stockings even in the summer heat. I was, in her eyes, a famous poet come to their house for afternoon lemonade by the pool. They'd seen my picture in the papers and had heard my name on the radio. I had a name in liberal circles and had given an interview about how

113

to write poetry. Levine kept praising me for the way I'd streaked down the pitch and fed the strikers with superb balls.

'Trotsky,' I said. 'His aunts still live in Jo'burg, the Bronstein sisters. My mother knew them well. What trouble we had with that boy, they used to complain, always in and out of prison, or on the run. Thank God he changed his name. Those famous pictures of him standing next to Lenin, they've gone. Stalin wiped out his image.'

How do you know that Levine didn't just put himself next to me in that picture of our first team? Was he ever in the first eleven?

'It's quite extraordinary,' I said when I left, 'but I don't remember you at all.'

I'd embarrassed him in front of his wife. What hatred and accusation came out of me, she was thinking what a nasty man to have brought to the house. I could see I'd frightened her. She was clutching her eldest, aged four, and allowed him to keep his thumb in his mouth. And when I laughed at them, trying to make out that what I'd just said was really a joke, they didn't believe me, which was quite right. I had not meant what I'd said as a joke. I simply couldn't stand another minute with that impostor.

I know, E., that you would immediately start talking about blocking out memory because of some overriding factor which might, if we found out, have nothing whatever to do with Levine. For some reason he was in my way and that's why I blocked him out. I grant you all that, but have this to add: memory rots. All my life I've assumed that memory holds for life, but that's not so. Meeting Levine taught me that, walking into this stranger whose existence I had obliterated at some time in the past. You have no idea what joy I derive from this, for next time I take a plunge into that darkness which has so often threatened to engulf me I shan't be afraid of letting go. I'll simply accept that the fruit in the orchard of my mind has not been picked, that some of it will fall to the ground and rot, and I'll survive the winter unscathed and blossom again next spring.

Twelve

The last miles of my flight to Paris I was suddenly aware I was going to the wrong place. For Annie to await my home-coming in London is what I wanted and I'd broach the subject of moving to England with her at the first opportunity. I was about to begin my literary career - this time, I promise, for real - and I wanted to mix with poets writing in my language. I'd have a fight on my hands with Annie for her to leave Jaulin, but the stifling effect of France on my work was too strong for me to give in. I had some new suits in my baggage, new shoes and a dozen shirts, but was wearing old clothes for the journey for comfort, and also so as not to expose my new wealth to ridicule in Annie's eyes.

She was there at the airport when I came through, not in the thronging crowd by the arrival barrier, but sitting at the back to await my appearance. As soon as she saw me she came out smiling to embrace me. I thought her approach was subdued, not the overt happy welcome I'd expected, and I put this down to the clumsy estrangement she might have felt, greeting one newly bereaved. You've been in touch with death and for a time people feel shy with you.

It was strange returning to the Cit de Coeur. I'd been frightened to go back to our room, and rightly so. When I arrived it felt as though I'd lived there once, but that someone, or more than one lot of tenants, had moved in after me and changed the place. If anything the place looked more drab than before, the chairs and tables looked rickety, the bed was about to collapse because of a leg that had snapped after one of our wilder scenes. The nail I'd hammered in had split the wood further, and now the wound looked open and ugly.

'Now what shall we do?' Annie asked after she'd put down one of the cases she'd helped carry upstairs.

I think she meant what she said. She took off her coat but made no suggestive moves to call me to her, fingering the buttons of her blouse in the way which endeared her to me, touching her skirt where it covered her thighs. She was looking for guidance from me.

She said she'd make a cup of tea though she didn't want any, but evidently changed her mind because she brought two cups to the table. Perhaps she'd meant only to ask what we should do with all that stuff I'd brought back, where, in a space so confined, we should put it all. Because when she sat down the expression on her face softened, and when I held out my hand for her she took hold of it. I know you can't hold hands for long, the fingers get cramped and the messages you can send with odd pressures are limited, but when Annie withdrew her hand to stroke her brow I felt we were parting, a feeling I'd had ever since we'd met an hour before. I tried to put that shattering prospect out of my mind by saying to myself: as long as it's not now. That's what we do to survive, hold on tenaciously to what we want, and face disaster later. All those days between when she'd said I miss you I'd preened myself with one object in mind, to lie in her arms. I got up and made her stand up to embrace her, and then gave her the bottle of perfume I'd bought for her. She unscrewed it and dabbed some on, then came close to me so that I could smell her. Then we undressed.

Listen to this, E., I can't tell my secrets to anyone else, or my dreams, lest they spy on me and find out more about me than I know myself. That's not a risk I'm prepared to take, as I told glum Bonzo when I saw him in Jo'burg. I did have several talks with that dumb creature but wouldn't bring him to Europe

116

because of his mouth. It curves downwards at the edges and he really does look glum. Besides, I told him, we get on far better at a distance. At times it feels there's so much consciousness about, the outlets can't cope, and I overflow. I feel high and marvellous with so much coming into me. Thank God that fucker Jung has really brought home to us the idea of the unconscious – what a scapegoat concept! I was perfectly all right, your honour, when I left the house, going off to the woods to chop some firewood. And then, when I saw that little girl in that pretty dress, bending over to pick up her ball which had rolled into the ditch, my unconscious took over and made me chop her to pieces. So you see, your lordship, it wasn't really me, but something not under my control which simply used my swinging arms, and the axe I was carrying, to commit this dastardly deed. And so the fellow gets away with murder! They put him in the bin and a few years later let him go. And another thing before I begin to tell you what's come so succinctly to my mind, God knows where from. I know none of the characters but feel I've known them for many years, ten at least, which they consider to be a generation. Ever since I met Levine and he confronted me with that picture of our football team, I've felt I have no right to deny anything that comes to my mind, that I'm not, in fact, the judge who decrees what is and what is not reality, that I'm simply the carrier of the pack on my back without questioning its contents.

It starts with a letter I received from Claire, which took only three days to reach me from Adelaide, Australia. I'd known Claire in London when I first moved to the Earls Court area eleven years ago. We'd met in a late night-shop and she'd smiled at me because I had identically the same items in my basket as she had, a carton of milk and a packet of cornflakes, and we started talking. She had a lovely voice, clear as a bell, a fine instrument for expressing mischievous innuendoes, and I walked her home two streets away from where I lived. I thought she'd ask me up to introduce me to some boy-friend she was living with, a neat way to stop me pursuing her further. But she stood firm on her heels when we got to her house, and smiled at me. I'd noticed her hands were exquisite, small with thin fingers, a touching sight when she put her purchases on the pay counter and took money from her purse and then struggled to open a plastic bag to put her two packages in. But now I saw her face to face for the first time, and her pretty mouth surrounded by flawless skin. She lived, she said, with her mother. She was going to have a bath and paint her nails and go to bed. There was no question but that we had established enough intimacy to kiss each other good-night, and when I reached for her face, her cheeks at least, she didn't move away and allowed me to kiss her mouth. She gave me her number before she went upstairs and I rang her the next night and we started to see each other all the time, and I became her first lover. She was seventeen and worked as a secretary to a group of doctors in Harley Street. Her mother had blue-rinsed her hair and wore lots of make-up. She was, I imagined, a tough widow who went out with buyers in the store where she worked, but Claire could cope with her all right and there weren't too many problems when she wanted to spend the night with me.

I've often thought that Shelley's inspired idea that poets are the legislators of mankind is great copy for advertising poets to girls. They become drawn to our world, to the idea that we sit there and brood until the moment comes when in a flash we pluck and cull ideas and words from somewhere under the tutelage of inspiration without trial and error, without crossing out a comma, and that this happens to us because we are a chosen breed. It worked quick as lightning on Claire, the attraction to the poet's world, and she became my ardent camp-follower to poetry readings and jamborees of that kind. And, of course, she admired my work, which I read to her and she typed for me. It made her feel, so she said over and over again, and when she didn't actually say it, holding back in case such repetition jarred, somehow it made her feel 'in wondrous ways', as they say in fairy-tales, that she was privy to a poet's heart and head, that behind some of my images, if only they knew, she herself lurked. I played games with her when she came too close, invented a wife and two children I'd left behind in Africa,

118

sketched my life for her in the place I'd come from, then filled out detail after detail and said, well, before long, I'll have to return and leave Earls Court. That particular game I kept up for two full days simply to hear her call me a rat when I confessed it was all lies, and to feel her smack my cheek, playful and painful, before she embraced me with such gratitude for having made her suffering come to an end that she would have submitted to anything I had in mind for giving her so much joy. I put my head between her legs and kissed her there, opened her up to get at that lobe of flesh to link her to heaven and then I climbed up her body to go wild inside her. We used to walk through the London parks, cross them from one side to the other, talking I forget now what about, but talking all the time, the distances were always too short before we reached the exits.

Ten years have gone by. She came to me one day after drifting about with me for a year and told me she was going to marry an Australian insurance assessor, and that she'd move to Adelaide with him. I don't think she'd known him for more than a fortnight. I'd been away for treatment somewhere, but I think that baboon mother of hers and an elder sister had pushed her into getting married. That sister, Claire had told me, was moving about in circles where she denied her mother's impoverished existence. She'd hyphenated another name to hers to fake the sort of background that might help sweeten her prospects. I'd seen her once, that smart cookie, and she me, and I've no doubt that after one look at me I was not on her list of eligible bachelors, either for her or for Claire. I saw Claire the day she left. Nothing, it seemed, had changed between us. It was as if she were being sent away by her parent to a boarding-school called marriage, but that we'd stay in touch and see each other during the holidays.

And that's what we did, even with such a distance between us. She writes to me every six months and sends a Christmas card, and once or twice I've written to her. She calls me a rat for not writing more often. Always in her letters there's some line

119

to express the permanence of her feelings for me, an unwavering love no matter what I'm up to, or, for that matter, what she's up to. All that, she implies, is below the level of feeling between us and therefore doesn't count. Her mother, she told me in one of her letters, has died. Her sister had been to the funeral and sent her a ring for an heirloom.

Three weeks ago another of her letters arrived. She wrote how acutely she missed me at times, that she should have decided to live alone if I didn't want to live with her, that she was not unhappy but simply dissatisfied because she could not take me out of her life. I too had been thinking about her when the letter arrived, and then it struck me that she was never far away, that whomever I was with she was there too, tolerant of my pursuits. I decided suddenly to break the distance between us and rang her. The line was quite clear and it was marvellous to hear her voice. After ten years I heard again that oscillation of e, the timbre of her voice. The distance between us, ten years and twelve thousand miles, was suddenly cut. I told her to come to England. I'd send her the ticket and she said she would come as soon as she could, that she'd have to think up a lie to tell her husband. I left that to her.

She came and we had three radiant days. She cooked simple meals and was thrilled to be back in London. She loved the lights over the city at night, something I'd also found, I remembered, quite special when I'd first arrived from Africa, and that haze in the London parks, a shimmer of blue and green. She spent quite some time on the phone trying to trace her sister who was, when last heard of, living in Biarritz. She rang Munich and Rome, and someone in a village in the Dolomites, and her search wasn't over when I found her lying on the floor. I'd been out to get a bottle of wine for our supper, I put it on the table and laughed at her prank. Ten years ago we'd played games like this, we'd collapse on the floor, or on the grass in the park when it was dark enough, and we'd not get up until at least we'd played with each other, or better still, made love. I started on her, holding her head and stroking the insides of her thighs, and suddenly I knew without putting my head on her breast that she was dead. It's not, you know, what you'd expect, people to die in the middle of nowhere. You, E., would pick up that word 'nowhere', because it's not quite the right one to use. But you'd know at once I used it because I was at that moment concerned with 'place' and not with romantic mishmash. Romance, in fact, lay dead on the floor. That's what I was concerned with. God, what a mess!

The first thing I did was to turn off the gas under the stew Claire had been cooking. I gave a forlorn look at the bottle of Burgundy I'd just purchased, I was beguiled by its innocent and clear appearance and the pleasure it held for the living, and then for some reason I can't explain I put a pillow under Claire's head. After that I don't think I touched her again. I thought of going through the yellow pages to find an undertaker to take Claire away and take care of things. Or of going down to Frau Eppstein to tell her what had happened. Being older than I was she was better versed in dealing with the dead. And that's just what I did. I told Frau Eppstein and she came up at once and took a look, just as she would have done had I reported a broken sash-cord or a leak in the sink. Oh, my dear, what to do, she said, asking the same question I'd asked myself, but at least there were two of us now to deal with the problem. Such a pretty girl - has she family here? No one, I told her, I'm the only person she knows in London. Oh, what a business, and so many things she has! Frau Eppstein had glanced at the various suitcases of Claire's, a lot for a short stay I'd thought when she had arrived, and she'd unpacked only one of the three, the others stood open on the floor, her clothes in meticulous folds because there was nowhere to hang her things. Good old Frau Eppstein took charge and went off to call a doctor. He'll manage things, she said, you need certificates when you are dead.

The doctor came and within and hour they took Claire away. I'd not got her private address, had had neither the time nor the inclination as yet to go through her handbag, so gave them the address I had of the office where she worked in Adelaide, and

121

that's what was stated on her death certificate. A nice touch, I thought, the rewards of working at a deadly job, doing the typing in some insurance office. Frau Eppstein and I discussed how best to inform Claire's husband. I went through her handbag looking for her home address and on my way to her little diary came across her compact, which I undid and held close to my face, a farewell to the mirror that had last seen her image. I undid her lipstick too and smeared some on the back of my hand, a kind of kiss I'd taken for granted had she still been alive. Somehow, I felt, I was defusing these delightful objects which had given me so much pleasure in the past. Give the address to the undertaker, let him deal with the next of kin, Frau Eppstein had advised in ticker-tape fashion. In her state of excitement, I'd noticed, she made no pauses in her speech.

I followed her advice and told the undertaker to inform me when the funeral would take place. Three days later they rang to tell me the cremation would be at eleven sharp the next day. I was horrified. Cremation, you know, is not a Jewish idea. We don't like things as final as fire, it's an insult that joker Eichmann must have found most amusing.

I didn't sleep that night I was so disturbed. I should have got rid of Claire's suitcases, but putting them outside my door wasn't far enough, and I thought of taking them down to the Embankment and throwing them into the Thames. But someone might have seen me do that, the river police might have fished them out and the law would have lurked behind some tombstone at the cemetery, and I could well have been arrested and accused of murder. So many things you cannot do in our society, like destroying the evidence of your lover because her pants and clothes prevent you from getting a decent night's sleep.

Imagine, E., I was the only one, apart from the resident vicar, who was in that chapel at Ealing. I'd half suspected Claire's husband might turn up and at first sat at the back, just in case. I'd never asked her whether she'd ever told him about me, but I suspect she had. Perhaps, though, my suspicion was wrong and brought about mainly on account of some paranoia which overcame me in that empty chapel. The vicar had beckoned me to the front and had shaken my hand, then asked me to sit near the coffin. As there were only the two of us I found his prayers moving. The 'us' in his versicles were he and I, and I felt close to him in his dispatch of Claire. Having pronounced her name and called her a daughter of the Lord, he pressed a button to make the coffin slide into the works behind. I should have brought Claire's suitcases along to ferry them into the fire after her.

Tell me, E., who is Claire? Some dream-creature I've summoned from my unconscious? In such detail? The nail of the big toe of her right foot had a blue patch, was discoloured because of the tightness of a new pair of shoes. There's lots more I could tell you about her, blemishes and points of radiant beauty, the skin between her breasts and shoulders, how when I kissed her there she lay disarmed by my side. Who was she? Take her and unfold my invention, reveal the chemistry of her existence. Why is she there, you dumb arsehole? You never respond when I need you, you mark time by scratching your cheek and then dive like Donne's flea up the elephant's trunk to itch the brain to distraction because of your inability to discover. You're a rotten navigator to take on a journey of discovery.

Perhaps I've felt the cracks on the earth I share with Annie and prepared myself for the great void of separation. That's how Claire had arisen, a phoenix from future ashes. I remember in late summer kicking the withered dandelions and running after the floating pollen. That's my first memory of the chase. And I remember Louise laughing when I opened my hand to show my catch. That's dead seed, she said, you've squashed it to death, little boy. I'm floating through the night with Annie next to me, she's fast asleep and has no idea of what goes on inside my head. I should like, E., to be the instrument of revelation, to be shown everything I am through him. Perhaps tomorrow night I'll chase Irma floating across the park. She's no doubt found that layer of air that will fill her umbrella with power to glide past me and I'll catch her and unfold my spoil to laughing

Louise. She did tell me when I arrived at home that she'd opened the window as soon as she found Maman dead, to allow her soul to fly off. Can I catch her, and will she not rise again elsewhere?

Thirteen

Annie has sat quietly, hardly speaking for three days. How much longer I can control my rage I don't know. I want us to move to London and she's showing, as I'd envisaged, a great deal of resistance. When I told her about my inheritance she was visibly shocked. She hadn't expected such an amount, and it acted on her like a barium meal being forced down her throat, though it needs someone more expert than I to read the X-ray. Money soon joins the board of your company, it's a partner inclined to interfere. It's interfering with me, I've not done a stroke of work since I've come back, and it's interfering with her too. That hunchback Jaulin has got her under his wing. She makes out, as if I didn't know better, that that Quasimodo has to be pushed around in a wheelchair, that's she's become his right hand, a situation, she miaows, she deplores but finds it so hard, don't you see, darling, to get away from? I wonder what else she does for him other than wheel him from one site to another. If he lay on his back he'd wobble on his hump like an upside-down camel. And if she lay beneath him she'd have to touch, sooner or later, that swelling on his back which has frightened us since childhood, for we suspect these humps to contain organs we don't possess ourselves. Then there's that one-armed bandit of a father. He's been so kind, buying her that car to wedge a distance between us, something, he told her when he handed her the key, to run away in. He's not been well of late, she feels, for the five minutes of every hour she considers our move, she ought not to leave Paris just now. She feels, I know, undecided as to which way to turn, there's a tug of war going on in her head between Paris and me, and I'm trying all the time to add weight to my side to topple her resistance. Bugger the architect and that decrepit *capitaine*! I'll use any trick to loosen her grip on the rope and pull her over. I've worn smart suits since I've returned, discarded my old togs as if I'd suddenly moved from childhood to manhood, and when I go outdoors I wear a hat, wide brimmed and of soft black felt. I've refrained so far from acquiring a dandy's walking-stick, as that would remind me too much of Mother's brollies. And Annie likes me that way, respectfully attired. I'm smart enough, she said yesterday, to be taken to see Papa, for suddenly my wealth is reflected in my outward appearance. Come, we'll split a good bottle and talk about my daughter now you've got proven assets. I won't go near that wet-farting Gaullist to bargain for his daughter. I know where I don't belong.

I've had a letter of condolence from Lothar. My brother had told him of Maman's demise when he saw him in Vienna. He wants to come and visit me in Paris. Another cripple in the baggage of people I know. I'm suddenly surrounded by them and feel I ought to start limping in sympathy. I'll put him off for a couple of weeks until we've settled in London. I can see flickers of submission coming from Annie; in the end she'll move. Jaulin is no Le Corbusier at whose feet you take part in history, he's just a nice man. *Il n'est point digne de commander me vie!* That's what she said when I stuck a few words sharp as scissors into his rump. Then she embraced me. You really are impossible, my pet. Flashes of victory I've seen, and though I don't wish to subtract one iota from Annie's love for me, I know too that money speaks. Our partner attends every meeting we have, is there all the time as if we were shrink-wrapped together. Annie is suddenly as tender as hell when we hit the hay, there's hardly anything left for me to seduce. I'm yours, my sweetheart pet, *mein Liebling*, my gifted man. I bet she's expecting that bird-call from me to marry her, that mothering desire has taken hold of her, that's how it's going to be, just one fuck and you won't know what's hit you, darling. A touch of blackmail keeps the human kind alive, till ring-a-ring o' roses we all fall down.

We go to London, yes? Annie asked two days later, after she'd got up and pottered around for a few minutes. I've told Jaulin I'll be leaving at the end of this week. I held out my arms from the bed, and she came up to me and let me embrace her around the top of her thighs with my head on target in front. She kept stroking my head, and with one move I could have made her come back to bed, but that didn't interest me for the moment. I never celebrate victories. At the point of arrival the journey is dead.

My new partner advised me to give up our attic because he knew I had no intention in future of returning to it. Much to his annoyance I overruled him. I needed that room for Annie to return to in case things didn't work out between us. Besides, I couldn't face saying adieu to Sabatine and looking at that unctuous smile she was bound to produce for such an occasion. Bravo, Mademoiselle, you've caught your fish at last. I'll pay the rent rather than look at her face.

We took the car, which was piled full with our things. We'd had a roof-rack fitted and the stuff on top was almost the same height as the car. The moment we reached the outskirts of London I felt at last that my work was going to blossom, that nothing could hinder me now from fulfilling my promise. I wound the window down as soon as there were people about to catch their sounds, odd words that might reach me. I'd asked my brother to find us a bigger place, though I was loath to leave Frau Eppstein's house. I'd had no reply as yet, there hadn't been time. I didn't look forward to Frau Eppstein's tears when I greeted her. She'd not be as matter of fact about Maman as she'd been about Claire. And I was right. I'm sorry, my child, she said the moment she saw me, about your dead mother. I'll miss her visits and our little chats together. Always about you she worried and gave me so many instructions. I always laughed. He'll be fine, I used to tell her. He's a big boy, my dear.

127

But she went on with her instructions just the same as if that was what mothers are for, to tell their children what to do, no matter. By the end of the week she could let us have two more rooms on our floor, people were moving out. That saved us looking for a new place.

I can't tell you what went on in my head, there's too much to tell. Like Hannibal's men I could smell the sea, but was too far away as yet to see the divide between land and sky. On top of Everest you imagine the world at your feet though you see but the peaks of neighbouring giants through your frozen eyes. After that arduous journey with mad intervals I felt that my frame was hard as stone protecting the fragile parts of my being, and that at last the leakages of hurt were stopped, that I was standing safely at the edge of art. I was bad company for Annie, I was preoccupied with the birth of work, wouldn't open my mouth for hours except to sip hot mugs of tea she provided from time to time. And though I was in this tumultuous state of creation, nothing, but nothing, came to me, that form and population I needed to flex my muscles against. What shall I do with all that food which will rot by tomorrow, the jugs of wine will turn into vinegar if the feast does not take place today? Mozart had symphonies in his head and copied them down whilst chatting to his wife. From one paragraph in a Dresden newspaper Dostoevsky drew inspiration to write *The Possessed*. I did doodles for two or three days. My pen wanted to work, so whilst I was waiting for creative action I filled in the time somehow. I wrote several pages, just words to fill the lines. I was ashamed Annie might catch me idling; she could see I was in a high state but calm underneath my frustration. Then, suddenly, I started. I don't know how the pieces came together.

*

There's a man called Death in our part of the world. The kids keep calling him that, that name which sticks to his reputation has been handed down to them and he'll never live it down. I've seen him myself umpteen times, all of us have who live in the neighbourhood. He's earned his nickname because of the fires and his blackened face. When he pushes his bike through the street, a cart on two wheels, children stop their games. Their heroes roll a ball into his path, and when they retrieve it they run back and boast how near they've been to Death.

It's hard to determine how old Death is, his hair might be a pointer to his age, but no one has ever seen it because he always dons a wide-brimmed hat which sits firmly on his head. And he wears a stout mac, unclean like his face, tightly belted. It's long and reaches below his knees. His bike is thirties' vintage, solid and slow, the way they made bikes in that era. He's always got items loaded on his vehicle, a tool-bag, planks of wood sometimes, strapped firmly to the frame, an expanding ladder it would take two to carry. He can be seen in all weathers repairing some house or other in the district. You can tell he's around working inside or at the back, if you can see his bike against the fence.

I got to know old Archer quite well the year he was painting the outside of Frau Eppstein's house, and she has filled me in with quite a few details, though there's much that remains a mystery. He's been a builder all his life, and at one time had three men working for him, but he didn't replace them when they grew old, as he couldn't find anyone else suitable for the meagre wages he paid. He lives a most frugal life and, from his diet Frau Eppstein once described, I can't see where he gets his strength from. The houses in our part of Earls Court are tall, four storeys at least, and he's painted many of them single-handed, from the gutters of the roof all the way down, and he's made a fair job of it. He is, of course, much in demand, for doing jobs like that without scaffolding saves hundreds of pounds. He talks only when it's essential, when he's cornered into opening his mouth, as the time he came past my open window when I was sitting at my desk, and our heads weren't but a yard apart. 'Morning,' he said. And that was all, as if he couldn't afford any more words whilst scaling the ladder perched at a steep angle.

It was the year I moved to Frau Eppstein's that the first of the fires occurred. Mr Archer lives round the back of our house. You can just about see the corner of his yard which is full of old doors and timbers and rusted drainpipes, an accumulation from years of gathering the broken fabric of our neighbourhood. The yard skirts his house, a grey Victorian building with a charming façade. You can still see it today in spite of what's happened. None of the newcomers to our neighbourhood had ever seen his wife. By the time we arrived she was an invalid confined to her bed. The fire was started by a spark from the burning stove, it's so easy when you burn moist timber, for it dries bits which tighten and curl, then suddenly snap and jump beyond the confines of the grate. I remember the acrid smell in the air, the stench of burning clung for days to the November air, caught hold of your clothes. It appears that the white smoke cavorted like playful dolphins into Mrs Archer's room and billowed down her throat until she was dead from suffocation. Nothing much else was damaged, for the old boy had been called and had driven back at his regular pace to put the fire out with a few buckets of water. It wasn't too cruel a death for a woman with a heart condition, a few coughs, perhaps, and then it was all over. That's what everyone said. It's not much of a life once you're confined to your bed and your husband turns out to be a bad nurse.

My enthusiasm to tell of this first conflagration has made me omit mentioning Archer's wealth. He is, in fact, the owner of several houses in our neighbourhood, where prices are high and rising. Three houses I know of are his, apart from this burnt-down dwelling. There were no signs of a fire about his house when his wife was destroyed, but there were when his roof burnt down a year or so later. I was not in London at the time, but was told that the flames rose high against the night sky. People saw Archer go in and out of his abode to retrieve whatever he could – some, it turned out, quite useless items he should not have bothered to keep in the first place. But such is our attachment to certain of our chattels, to what we have acquired in one way or another, that it is unfair to judge whether a footstool or a tattered hat is worth risking one's life for by drawing aside a curtain of flames to re-enter a house. It is said that people saw Archer's silhouette several times, that he slipped through the cordon of firemen quenching the thirsty flames, and that every time he emerged with some pathetic possession, scalded like a hare racing through a burning cornfield. On that occasion the roof and upper floor were set to ruin, and the floor below was spoiled beyond belief by water and the collapsed fabric from above. After months of arduous labour he repaired the roof with corrugated iron, a temporary job, we all thought, whilst he lit fires to dry off the soaked remains of his possessions. He was insured all right and presumably his claim was settled, and he must have simply pocketed the money. That's what the chemist lady reported, the woman who dispenses our prescriptions in the neighbourhood and knows a great deal about us all.

In one of his properties lives a spinster of retired age. She occupies the ground floor and basement of a pretty house in our best tree-lined street. The observant person, I've recently discovered, can easily tell which are the three Archer properties, for they're all painted the same colour, a tasteful beige, and the front doors black. It appears that old Archer, and this is why he's still tolerated after his incendiary adventures, is a decent landlord who doesn't charge nearly enough rent to his tenants. One may surmise from this that quite simply he's out of touch, or that repairs don't cost him more than they did twenty years ago, less, in fact, since, as I say, he's abandoned his work-force and now does everything himself. I imagine, if he could be drawn on the subject, he'd reveal himself as a man who's against society, one who'd be averse to accruing more rent which would result in paying higher taxes. Also, a man needs to find kindness in the world. Archer's benevolence is rewarded by the respect of his tenants, though he does not seem to notice that this overt esteem is also a cover for their fears. As they pay such low rents, unique, perhaps, on the London market, they are also reluctant to ask him for essential repairs, and I know of one roof he's inadequately attended to which had to be repaired eventually at the tenant's expense, as the leak was completely spoiling one of her rooms.

That spinster, well past her sixties, is a pretty lady. At one time, I'm told, she lived with a female companion, but for years now she's been on her own and the front room which her companion occupied stands empty. This is common knowledge in the neighbourhood. Miss Lampert should never have removed the curtains of her empty room for their annual clean and then not put them up again, exposing to everyone that her front room stood empty, for news like that spreads like a malignant growth on the body of gossip. She's talked about now, Miss Lampert, and there are several opinions about that third and final fire which occurred just before we came back from France. There's nothing left now of Archer's house but the façade and the rubble behind, and the yard is in even more of a shambles than before.

There are some who say that old Archer is the victim of social neglect, that an old man like him should not have been allowed to carry on living in a decrepit abode he had no will to rebuild. There are homes for the old and infirm. But other tongues wag differently. They don't put it past the old devil to have planned all these fires, for convenience and greed and getting his way. After the last fire there was a wave of compassion for him, people are said to have seen this forlorn figure bereft in front of his broken house, and to have offered him cups of tea and an old coat or two to make do with. Rather than blame himself for what had happened, he was cursing the fire brigade for their rough handling, for hacking their way through the remains of his house to put out the flames until there was virtually nothing left. And nosy Miss Lampert, that diffident spinster, she got up early that day to watch the disaster from her window at the back. She stood there for two hours, fearful that sparks might fly over and ignite the Tree of Heaven in her garden. When that danger passed she painted her face and walked round to take a proper look at Archer's ruins.

'Are you all right, Mr Archer?' she asked.

'I was just coming round to see you. I'd like to move into that front room you're not using. I'm sure you won't mind. Been empty for years, and I'll bring my mattress round. Got a spare set of keys? God knows where mine are in all this.'

Miss Lampert was so taken aback by the affront that her mouth stood open, and drawing her breath she attracted a bit of floating ash the wind had swept up. She caught it on her tongue, thought it was a fly which had flown into her mouth by mistake, and went after it in an unladylike way with her fingers, smudging her lipstick. 'Yeah . . . yes, of course,' she heard herself say – or who was it said this? she asked herself. I'll fetch the keys right away.'

'That's all right, then. I shan't be a bother.'

The cynics amongst us laughed when they heard of Archer's cheeky approach to Miss Lampert. I must say it immediately threw quite a different light on Archer's incendiary adventures. I know I was not the only one churning out theories about Archer's misfortune. Most people, though, presumed that the first fire was an accident and that the next two were simply the dragnet of fate which makes up the proverbial figure three. I thought otherwise. I'd always been on the side of the children taunting that nasty creature stalking our streets and calling him Death. Why, your lordship, for thus I argued my case in court, did the accused ride back at his ordinary slow pace, why didn't he get a move on when he was told there was smoke coming from his house, which, by the time he'd got back, had killed his wife? Was he not sufficiently concerned about this bedridden woman to have moved at top speed? When asked by the judge why indeed he'd been somewhat unconcerned as indicated by his slow pace, the old devil gave a most plausible answer. I was taught by my father and mother, he said, to take things as they come, and to avoid panic. And who could gainsay evidence like that? Stupidity, stubbornness and parental teachings are a state of mind the law cannot challenge. But I, Archer, know better than that. I put it to you. The first fire was murder. I think you fuelled that fire with consummate skill, the flue adjusted so that the damp wood would snap with tiny explosions, the sound of crackling sending shivers up the invalid's spine, heat and cold which the mind translates into anguish and fear, and then the billowing smoke when the damp carpet caught fire, the smouldering chewing the fabric and spewing out smoke like nasty breath. I think you had your eye on Miss Lampert for years. In your lonely mind you became quite a poet about your life, and formed a definite internal structure with Miss Lampert, a crystal if not of love, of longing at least. And my God you've come an ugly route to your goal. You want to croodle to that fallow spinster, but you'll find a dry nest when you get to it, every bone in her will ache with terror at your approach. Will you put her on your bike, that life-size doll, and push her around the neighbourhood, Death and the Maiden on wheels? And that sly smile which worms across your mouth when you acknowledge someone in the street, what exactly is the meaning of that? Oh unctuous man, things have changed. At one time they looked upon you as that shy, sad man saddled with a crippled wife, you weren't getting it anywhere and had to accept your fate as one of the smitten on this earth. Perhaps you took your bank statements to bed and fondled the figure of your fortune rather than some warmer creature. But now that smile is far more sinister, once more you'll pocket the insurance money on the sly and claim possession of Miss Lampert's apartment and turf her out, or else cohabit with an unwilling partner. Or is she too in the plot for some financial reward, your fire-moll? Tell me, Death, tell me all, you know how curious we all are about you.

Frau Eppstein says Mr Archer will marry Miss Lampert before the year is out. It's inevitable, she says, impossible for a man to live in your apartment and no hanky-panky, just you wait and see. She saw Miss Lampert at the bakers the other day, buying enough for two, then followed her, quite perchance, to the butcher's, where she purchased two chops. She's feeding her man, you can tell. I don't know why Miss Lampert doesn't go elsewhere for her shopping, so as to avoid the gossiping tongues, the weird looks and lewd remarks the moment her back is turned. She's become, Frau Eppstein remarked, a bird hopping from shop to shop foraging for food to take back to her nest. Frau Eppstein is quite amused by it all. So am I, but for a different reason. I don't think anything good will come from Death, it never does. He'll end up licking Miss Lampert into shape, or else start another fire and let the flames do the licking.

It goes without saying that that sly old fob stalks our neighbourhood just as before. Some people expected a change once he'd moved in with Miss Lampert, but there was none. His face has stayed grimy, his mittened hands show black talons grip the handlebars as he pushes his bike along. Perhaps his body is lily-white and he washes himself clean when he comes indoors, and in the morning he blackens his face to play Death in our streets. For how can he suddenly appear a gallant before our eyes, sport new clothes and shoes without casting suspicion that his Othello is in fact the treacherous Iago who tricked his darker half to commit murder? Not in his lifetime will Death live down his grisly past.

*

My room is at the back, overlooking the back gardens. They're a miserable sight, nobody seems to have green fingers around here. Nothing thrives but a few bushes and trees which need no attention. It's one of the new rooms Frau Eppstein has allotted us, and I've chosen it to be mine because it's the quietest room in the flat. Though two floors up you hear little noise from the street, so my choice of room here is concerned more with isolation than with noise. Annie is making attempts at bourgeois existence. Every day she brings patterns back to the house, and she asks me to help choose the furnishings we're buying. I let her direct our choice and am not concerned with what she buys, though she insists on making every purchase a sharing, an act of togetherness, and she's quite unaware how I detest these murmurs of settling down, or the ensuing comfort which injects poison into a striving mind.

I want my room to be slightly cold, almost bare but for a table to work at and a simple chair, a few shelves for books. It need never be cleaned, in fact I want no one to enter to disturb the solitary spirit of the place. I have pictures on the wall, that charming *La Femme-Rose* with Marie-Claire's blossoming head, and one of Chaim's views of Cagnes – it's so fat and thick with colour that I want to eat the canvas, to satiate my hunger at a glance. The blank walls come alive and depend on my beaming vision. Yesterday Marie-Claire walked through those ochre streets of Cagnes, down to the beach where Pablo was waiting. He was angry with her, what a temper he has, for being late, but then he calmed down when she told him Soutine had made the village slippery with his paint, it was hard to walk. I tell myself too many stories by half. I can't sustain repetition, to start out from the same house every morning and return there at night. That's not for me. I miss Mama to run away from, and am frightened that before long I'll turn Annie into that surrogate beast whose clutches and flapping wings I dare not allow to touch me, so that I must run away when she approaches me. Help me, explain, E., that oscillation between love and repulsion, it has to do with that dual function of the cunt, love to come in and poisoned waters to exude. You just sit there and listen to my pleading, not one word of guidance comes my way. If I deducted all those dumb moments from your fees you'd owe me a fortune, you arsehole. I want to know what I'm going to do between three and five this afternoon, I have to write a poem I'm going to recite at a poetry reading, I'm billed as one of the stars and am ashamed of everything I've ever written, and you, I can see your momentary hesitancy, because by now you know how I detest repetition, are going to play that same fucking record of birth and, as a *bonne-bouche*, pre-natal life – oh well, hm, it all has to do with your emergence from the womb, for nine months you were boss until the placenta burst and she told you to get out. And then your mother, instead of holding you close to her when you appeared, asked whoever was near to take you away. Clean that creature up, I couldn't possibly touch him like that, and bring him back in an hour or so after I've had a rest, and then I'll see what I can do about a feed. What a whore! The moment you've had your fun she tells you to get out and, what's more, threatens to make you pay for all the pain you've caused her and the mess you've made of her body. Bonzo is monstrous at times, the way he squats and makes me see Annie crouch with her pants down when that's the last thing I want to see.

Fourteen

Hullo, this is the captain speaking. Madame Parapluie taught me to speak with that same confidence with which she was taught deportment by that sexy aunt she often talked about, the one who, with manicured fingers, as she pulled an ace from her bridge hand, declared in her accented English, I'm putting my arse on the table. It's nice to know that Maman has returned as my sparring partner, that my ability to rail against her has recovered from the temporary impotence caused by her death, that when things have gone wrong I've already been able to call her 'that Mengele fucker' several times, with my anger modulated to perfection.

And things have gone wrong. Schloss sent me five thousand pounds to last me for four months and Annie has spent half of it in three weeks. Our rooms now sprout flower-patterned chintz and I asked her the other night whether she was watering the furniture to grow such hideous flowers. She burst into tears and was so angry that she walked out of the house, banging the door behind her, then returned half an hour later to prepare supper. She's laying foundations for our bourgeois life in London, the carpets, I feel, are taking root, and before long she'll go all soft and broody and then she'll grow really angry because of my indifference to her bird-calls, all that cooing and trickery of the womb. If that brolly-bitch has taught me one thing it is to beware of that female treachery which for one squirt of pleasure forces you to settle down. I'd tear up that recipe, Annie, if I were you. It's not a dish for a wandering Jew.

They liked that poem of mine the other night, though they laughed so much at my clowning theme that I doubt whether the subtlety of my piece drove home: Lolita in search of dead souls, using as her means of transport a London bus with Chichikov at the wheel. That clever lecher Humbert Humbert was with her. When he boarded the bus Lolita asked him to remember which side he dressed, implying the joy of bus-rides for old men which gives them the touch of the horn without being touched. Lolita's favourite stretch of Chichikov's ride was when they crossed the bridges which girdle the Thames – 'They corset the river,' she taunted the old boy, as she watched him pant and hold on for dear life. But old Humbert Humbert was wise to the child, held on to her thigh, and as they turned a corner gained access to her lighthouse and she felt the waves of raging London bash against her. Oh, marvellous supplication as she lay on the floor with old Humbert Humbert stuck inside her whilst that mad Russian made the bus dance like a Cossack through the London traffic. I should have made that poem very much longer but had only an hour to write something to read that night. I'd always thought that Chichikov and Humbert Humbert would get on well together, and they downed a bottle of vodka after the reading whilst I went home with Annie.

I'll not, before long, be able to keep Annie at bay. Her rollers, I think, are mid-Atlantic by now and will swerve towards my shore high and powerful, carrying shoals of disaster in their wet belly which she'll spew at me. I'll have to keep my head above water or else be absorbed by that powerful female, the sea. I can't help but call on Joseph to interpret my dreams, and half-way through, that beautiful man with a red beard and deep blue eyes, and hands to beguile a king, turns into that jackbooted villain whom my mother harassed with her yodelling cunt. It's not good to be stuck between good and evil, construction and destruction, whatever opposites you care to think of. Talking about keeping your head above water, if the height of your body is normal, an inch is luxury for me. I sniff near the ground like a dog and am assaulted so often by the rubbish I come across, which I usually lick before rejecting it. I could fill a book with mementoes of love for Annie, words I've written are like stars of nights I remember. I know stars are there for ever, but for me my awareness of singular moments is branded on my firmament. Or half-sentences no one but I can make sense of, pour them into that pot of love and you'll see a turmoil which turns into still and thriving waters, a Galilee of miracles. Here's one such half: I want every day to be there. . . . The rest stayed locked in my head, but here it is: when Annie puts on her mascara. Such longing is the ink with which taboos are written on the Torah of the heart and which you read over and over again until, is it, the end of time? But similarly there are points of disjunction, cracks which widen on that dangerous mountain, your feelings can no longer get a grip and crash to death. It's foe or friend dictated to by weird chemistry. Sometimes I look at Annie with enemy eyes, it's as if I've solved her for my needs and have no further use for her. But a moment later she once more enchants me, and those rats which gnawed at my love scurry from my head, leaving my eyes sore, as if those creatures had rummaged about my sockets, that's what it feels like.

Lothar arrived three days ago, it's all very disturbing. I've not been too well for a week, it feels like measles inside me, I itch all over although my skin is clear. We've been smoking a lot. Annie is on one of her insatiable kicks with the stuff – this time, I think, to impress Lothar, teaching him the art of rolling a joint and giggling a great deal at his attempts with the unruly tobacco and paper, and giving the names of animals to those pricks he turns out, worm, caterpillar, salamander. He is enchanted by her. They're as intimate as favourite cousins and play like children together. I've had dreams the past few nights featuring insects. The floor was carpeted green and turned out to be a wave of locusts which were roused the moment you trod on them. And the picture I was looking at, a nude female with crawling bees on her, the signature a snake. They all started to follow my roving eye and were alive, and when they reached her mouth she opened it and let those creatures inside. It has, I am sure, to do with my itching skin. I am most uncomfortable.

Lothar's presence disturbs me. When he came through that door it struck me how handsome he was. He's just that bit older than when I last saw him, his face is now at its best. His dark hair is luxuriant, his steel-blue eyes are alert and have lost that haze of youth, he's most engaging to be with. I asked him whether he'd brought his gun, though I could think of no adventure in England for which he might need it, and he said, half smiling, and faintly nodding his head, that he had, yes, it was in his suitcase. Then he laughed. Perhaps he sensed I was frightened. Behind his jovial and now so confident manner there's still, I feel, that ruthless streak which sends missiles of shivers through me when I look at him. My fear points to his leg, and I ask myself what it must be like to be attacked and not be able to kick back, not be able to run out of the house if that firebrand Archer decides to play one of his jokes and boil Frau Eppstein in her bath. He'd make you carry him to safety at the point of his gun.

Lotharre has become a swinging sound for Annie. The *Lo* shoots from the perfect circle of her mouth, and the lobes of her lips become so seductive that I twitch every time I hear her say his name. *Lotharre*, she calls out, the *r* finding taste-buds on the roof of her mouth which delight her. She seems all the time to snuggle up to him, with so much decorum as to make it seem imperceptible, but I notice all right. Again it's his stiff leg that focuses my attention. He sports it when he sits down, sticks it straight out in front of him, a victim's advert. She's always on the point of caressing him, of tucking him in whatever he's about, making him comfortable and licking his withered limb, if not like a docile bitch to extract some favours from her master then with cushioned words which eliminate all harshness.

Ma brochette, I'll call him. You like that? she said to me the other night, in front of him. Look how soft his skin is, so *souple*, as if he had no bones. Her accent, always charming, is more pronounced when Lothar is around. She's making the best of being a Parisian, it's an attractive label on her suit of armour. Most nights when we're together in bed I funnel endearments

141

into her ear to make her deaf to Lothar. After I'm spent I don't think of him.

She entertains our house guest every day and her planned itineraries keep him occupied, and, I bet, amused! The Zoo, the Tower, a trip to Hampton Court, proper tourist stuff which is fun on summer days. They return in the late afternoon with mementoes of their visits, proofs where they've been, too good, I feel at times, to be true, and when Annie invites me to share in all they've done that day I feel remorse for my suspicions, for the hours I've wasted that day on mistrust for the eruptions of love I suspected which would exclude me from their bond.

Lothar sleeps late, which allows Annie and me to get dressed long before he wakes, and to spend the first hours of each day on our own. As a rule I grab those hours for my work, but since Lothar's arrival I've had to invest that time in keeping abreast with our privacy. We do nothing much, just sit around and read the papers and make odd comments when one of us spots an item the other might miss. We're both amused by printer's errors and read aloud the fuddled sentences, and Annie is often occupied with bits of sewing, she has taken endless trouble over some curtains she has made for one of the rooms, and repaired some cushion covers she bought in a street-market, a new addition to our nest. I like those very ordinary things, being calm under one roof, disengaged and doing things together. I keep allowing Mama to have a look-in, see how nicely we've appointed our household, how well we live together, anybody could ring our doorbell and come in to find us clean and proper, members of the bourgeoisie. That I allow Mama to peep at us is kindness itself, but before long I can't help sticking my boot in with a touch of abuse. It's her money which is that soft cushion I sleep on at night, though money robs what money cannot buy, and I miss those patches of being cold in Paris and the need for dope which enlarged our sparse accommodation. And then, mid-morning, Lothar appears and Annie immediately leaves me to fuss over him, and I start itching with discomfort.

Every day I see that boyish smile when he comes in wearing his dressing-gown over his trousers. He laughs for no apparent

142

reason, probably because he feels vaguely guilty it's so late in the day, and Annie has to make fresh coffee to get him going. He wears trousers to hide his bad leg. I've never seen the brace which enables him to walk with a swinging limp. Within minutes that tart is all over him, she brings me another cup of coffee without asking whether or not I want it, and then sits at the table with Lothar and feeds the toaster with slices of bread until he says no more. It's that giggling they do which most disturbs me. I don't understand what provokes this. There are things she has kept private which have left me standing outside the door. I'm glad when at last they go off on their jaunt and I don't have to watch their body language any more, though when I start reciting it in my mind it does at times get worse. It depends on my powers of concentration that day how far I can distance myself.

What's so frightening is that Lothar's presence in our life has stirred up a hornets' nest. There's a constant buzz of anxiety as I witness Annie's behaviour towards a rival, though he may not be one. On whom will those hornets settle, whom will they disturb with their feather-light crawl? It's as if, suddenly, someone has come along and dropped a coin into that juke-box Annie and pressed for a tune I dislike, or a song I didn't know Annie knew which makes her swing her hips in a way I'd never seen before, as if she were humming from her pelvic girdle. And before I know where I am, the hand of jealousy with its fingers in every pie grips the back of my neck and turns my head to make me see what I don't want to see, nothing but falsehood in that smiling face, her skin roughens before my eyes, what she says is nothing but repetitions of what she's been on about all week, and she'll go on like that until she comes across some new minuscule concept which will engage her mind. It's like watching her masticate, I'm suddenly aware she's eating future shit! Or else my rage is set to kill Annie. It's all, isn't it, E., on account of that yodelling shyster, those phallic brollies she used either to penetrate or to open up and receive? She had the best of both worlds with that tool of her life. I've not forgotten when I touched that gun in Lothar's car, that cool, pear-shaped

143

handle with its snug trigger, *boom, boo boo boom*, one round to kill and four to record victory. Six rounds, Lothar said, so there'll be one left over, but it won't be for me. I shall want, for some time at least, to savour peace.

I've found the gun. At first I was most reluctant to look for it because my memory of it in Lothar's car carried messages that one day I'd like to pull the trigger. But four days ago things got so out of hand that I simply couldn't resist it any longer and went through Lothar's bag, where I found it wrapped in one of his shirts. What happened that day was most likely quite innocent, though now I'm not so sure.

Annie rang around six-thirty, more than an hour after their usual return, and said they didn't feel like coming home, they'd stay in town to see a movie and have something to eat afterwards. 'Had a good day?' she then asked.

'Yeah, great.'

'You're not angry, are you?'

'Course not.'

'Only we went to the Zoo, Lothar adored the mountain goats – he watched them for such a long time, I had to drag him away to visit my favourite cobra. He said you would understand about the goats. We'll be back around midnight.'

She could have added 'my pet', or 'sweetheart', or 'wait for me'. But she'd not rung to give me a message like that, just a cold piece of information, and she was surprised my voice was dead on the line.

'*Allô*, Fabrice! You still there?'

'Yes, I heard.'

'Then why do you not answer?'

'What's there to answer? Yes, I'll put a hot-water bottle into Lothar's bed and the oil-can on his table so that he can grease his joints when he comes in, unless you'd like to do that for him.'

'Oh, God!' she said, and then she had the nerve to put the phone down on me.

The next hour or so I expected them to come home, my mood having been reported to Lothar and Annie suggesting that

144

they'd better get back. I'd worked out how long it might take them, with ten minutes either way, and when it was twenty minutes beyond my estimated time for their return I knew I'd once more made a fool of myself. Annie had paid no heed to my mood and had carried on with that she wanted to do, and I admired her for her spirit and forgot my anger. I felt good, virtuous even, when I sat down to write six excellent lines of a new poem, after which I prepared three cups and saucers and ground some coffee in readiness for their return. Then I waited, reading once more the day's papers, I simply wasn't in the mood for a book at that time of night.

They weren't home by two o'clock. The first hour after midnight was still bearable. Every noise in the house, though there was hardly any and I had to strain my ears to pick up a sound, called for a bet I'd take with myself that that was them. Anxiety becomes subdued by diversion, and for an hour or so I succeeded in forestalling any anger. After that it spilled over. I'd played out every excuse I could think of for their non-return until that gravity which held my mind in orbit was destroyed and my thoughts went berserk like kites in a storm. With one swipe I broke the cups I'd put on the low table, and for good measure I smashed the jug against the wall, and the ground coffee on the carpet looked so much like ants that for a time I watched them move, then trod on them. I thought of clearing up the mess so as to remove the evidence of my anger, even of replacing the cups and putting out another jug and going to bed, so that Annie might be moved at least by the third cup and made to feel guilty about her nocturnal jaunt. Or I could leave a note, saying that the third cup was for the holy ghost who'd gone to bed to do some haunting. She doesn't like cracks about Jesus, that goy.

I was about to go to her cupboard and tear up her clothes, then thought I'd take some scissors to cut bits off. A propitious snip here and there can make any garment unwearable. I opened the wardrobe and took some stabs at skirts and dresses when suddenly it was as if the room were alive. I heard her scream at me, her hysterical voice made every bottle and stick of make-up

145

fall over on her dressing-table, and her hanging clothes started to move as if her body by some trick of transmutation were wearing all her stuff at the same time, her arms and legs making every movement they were capable of. I was in a whirlwind of rage and heard her shrill cursing. Seconds later, perhaps as long as a minute, there was calm, absolute stillness. The window was open, I'd expected foul weather outside, but it was calm and warm, and I think I saw old Death on his roof fixing his chimney in the moonlight. I'm not certain, though, for the travelling clouds were playing tricks with the light. Perhaps old Archer was lying on his couch, a ladder rising from his head, our Earls Court Jacob.

At half-past two I heard them come in. They were talking in whispers, though they didn't manage to lower the pitch of their laughter. I imagined Annie had thrown off her shoes and exposed her painted toenails shimmering through her nylons. That sent butterflies to my stomach. I was hard at the thought of her, and no matter at what time she'd join me in bed I'd get on top of her. A nice prospect that, which calmed me down and enabled me to lay my anger to rest and to play my part, which was simply to pretend being asleep. I'd be able by stealing a look to fill my delight in her by watching her undress, that marvellous unsheathing I enjoy so much. She was talking to Lothar. There's time before going to bed, late at night, the world's asleep, to relate parts of your life. Tomorrow I'll know things I needn't have known, that exploration wasn't worth the candle, or I'll be nearer to you than ever.

Papa has an 'orrible twitch on account of the explosion 'e lost 'is arm. I'm used to it now, it's quite amusing. I lurve my papa, 'e always makes me cut 'is meat when I'm there. The only time 'e misses 'is arm, 'e says, is when 'e eats meat, so 'e's glad to 'ave a daughter who will cut it for 'im. *Il est drôle, mon papa.*

I heard it all, for I'd crept out of bed and had opened the door a bit wider to hear them talk. Lothar must have complained about his leg, that's why she had volunteered the bit about her father. But you are strong, I heard her say, you walk so well, we walked miles tonight. I had no idea you could manage, you were

146

wonderful. The sheets against my lusting prick saved me from being sucked once more into that whirlwind playing havoc with my senses, for don't imagine I didn't think of some dingy hotel they'd gone to, Lothar having told her the story of some film that was showing at present, one I knew she hadn't seen before, to prime her with what to say when they got back. What upset me a moment later, when my lust was no longer sustained, was that my suspicion had been justified, that Annie was fascinated by Lothar's crippled leg which evoked her sympathy to serve him. I reasoned: if it's weakness she goes for to show off her strength, then there's no better way for a fellow with a gammy leg to get her than to expose his rotten limb as much as possible. And that Lothar certainly did. It satisfies, I hit on, her desire to mother. That cooing sound she's been directing at me has found an evening's answer, has transformed Lothar's visit into a keepsake neither of them will soon forget.

Shortly after she came to bed she told me of their long march. You know, my pet, she said, we'd run out of cash and had to walk all that way. You feel most vulnerable walking through London with only threepence on you. Perhaps my suspicions were unfounded after all. For how could she have made love like that a second time that night, pretended with such mastery as she enveloped me that I was her only man?

Fifteen

I don't think Lothar knows what he's doing, or what Annie is up to with him. It's three weeks now since he's arrived and there aren't any signs of his leaving. Before long I'll have to tell him to go. I've been on the point of doing so several times, but have restrained myself because of the effect this might have on Annie. In the end, though, what she thinks won't affect me.

He's at a loose end. He and I have discussed his life several times, and on some levels he's open with me, on others he's as tight as a clam. He's dissatisfied with his roots, wants to belong but doesn't feel he does, a common enough Austrian failing which made even some decent people embrace the Anschluss as if Germania were offering her tits like some Mother Earth. I've no idea how Lothar makes a living, he's certainly not short of cash, and in any endeavours to pry into his activities I've come up against a blank wall. Business, he says, occasional business. What sort of an answer is that? It's not so different from the answers Mama used to give when she was asked to explain her mooching about in London or Zurich. And there are other connections between that dead cow and Lothar. His leg is like her brollies, a decoration to be displayed, a sign of recognition. A shame that because of her disdain for his Nazi family she never met the fellow. She punished Alban because of his mother's SS connections, and now Lothar is punishing me because of his father. I'm being attacked, that's what it feels like, out of the blue. And to bear it and prepare my defence I have to seek the reasons behind it all.

I've talked to Annie about Lothar's extended stay, and she playfully dismissed my complaint. 'Why should you mind him, *chéri*? He's a nice companion for me whilst you're stuck in your study doing your writing, and he eats with such moderation I've hardly to buy extra food. I do like *ma brochette* - please let him stay, darling, *mon petit* pet.'

When she puts it like that, of course, I cannot object. She's such a cat, that woman, she comes purring up to you and lets you touch her, her back yields to the strokes of your hand, and all the time she can flit off any second to find amusement elsewhere. It's in her nature, you cannot talk about that, the needles of love at times miss those veins they're supposed to hit, and the only way to avoid this is to eviscerate that cat, spread her entrails on a slab and search for that evasive chemical which drove you crazy, which made you hunt after her as long as she lived. Such Mengele thoughts she evokes, for that's what he did with Jews.

I've had a frightening thought. For a time, you know, you hold a view of someone in the hand of your brain, and then you turn it and look at it from the other side, or half-way to there, and you suddenly see some glaring imperfection you omitted noticing before. How could Lothar sustain himself for three weeks without a woman? Confronted every day by that sexy cat, watching her feline movements, the twists of her delicious mouth, her flawless legs, and the stance of her pretty feet in high-heeled shoes, that as well as the warmth with which she receives his radiant admiration, his progress towards her as I discerned, how was it possible that on their daily outings they'd not found a bed to fuck on? It's easy to feel like a hawk watching from on high tiny creatures it will pounce on noiselessly from angles its verminous victims cannot perceive. I've watched Lothar like this, followed him in my sights for one give-away gesture, a scratch, a bite-mark, a patch on his neck where her saliva had dried, so precious that almost invisible stain that he'd not washed it off. But they just went on and on whipping my suspicions to race faster, then took away the winning-post and made me run to exhaustion.

I'll not be calm again. How can I be? Every time, it seems, I get my strength back, the wasps inside me start to agitate and are drawn to those four eyes which are like saucers filled with sugar-water Mama made Louise put on the veranda table to attract those stinging creatures. They rope me in, those wasps, to their greedy pursuit and set my skin abuzz.

E.'s not available to me, that shitpan. When I was still seeing him he used to tell me he'd be available at any time even after I'd stopped seeing him regularly, but that money-grabbing prick's not rung me back. I tried three times at the beginning of the week to get hold of him, rang him bang in the middle of his breaks between sessions, but he didn't come to the phone, and I left messages with his wife to which he's simply not responded. Perhaps my bin-shrinks in Paris and London have warned him off. Or my late mother gave him a mouthful when she sought his help in having me certified for a limited period when I was completely out of sorts on account of some rejection by one of our literary editors, which in turn made the girl I was with at the time leave me for someone else. Green-eyed Liz took her eyes round the corner when I came after her and ran out of the house where her friend, that big illiterate thug, was waiting for her.

I wanted to see E. on account of some of the dreams I've been having. They were so recurrent that I hardly know whether or not they were dreams at all or some other form of consciousness or unconsciousness. It's that old and persistent plague of females in my youth, and my obsession with their garments, which is so strong. It makes me feel a freak. Mama told Louise after a visit to Frau Horngrad's salon that she'd sleep in her new corset to get used to it, and it to her. And the way these women adjusted their suspenders when I was as high as their thighs! I saw it all, their pink underwear and their tight, flesh-coloured stockings, when the wind played tricks and raised their skirts, or when I played with marbles and made one of their high-heeled shoes my target so that I could creep up to it and take a peep higher up. It's left me, no doubt, with a desire at times to

150

be like them, to dress like them but to remain me. That's the feeling I get, that I'd like one of these women to dress me in their clothes, to teach me what to feel and to punish me if I didn't obey. For two days last week I was in that state where I was acting all the time, feeling my pants sheathe me, not crossing my legs the better to show them off, making effeminate gestures when I touched my face so as not to spoil my rouged cheeks and lips, though nobody, I bet, noticed my masquerade, nor did they see Frau Horngrad follow my every step, seeing to it that I sat on the toilet when I peed, prodded me to hold my head high with confidence, that pieces of food I put in my mouth were small enough so as not to smudge my lips. I felt afterwards that I'd had a recession from anger, that moving as I did like a female towards Annie, Lothar's encroachment of her had little effect on me for two days. I saw him for what he was, a young Viennese colt with a broken hoof.

After that short spell of remission my anger once more started to ooze out of me like a fever, as if my hormones had resettled after their desperate excursion. I was obsessed with what Lothar would wear the next day, whether he'd disturb the shirt he'd wrapped his gun in. I had my eye on it but dared not go to the drawer in case this time for certain I'd pull the trigger. I tried, my God, to stay within the bounds of reason. So hard I tried, my body was raw, I'd been stripped and covered with ants. Their mandibles bit off every hair on me, then started on my skin. Even after the baths I took their gnawing continued, and still I tried to hold on.

Listen. You remember that death-head Bender saying that I'd wanted to join in the fun, marching with the Hitler Youth through Vienna in a brown shirt and short pants held up by a belt with the Nazi buckle? Maybe he was right. At that time I became plugged into cruelty, which has since gained perpetual motion in me. Maybe E. was also right, pointing his finger at Mama who established that circuit inside me which took to cruelty as easily as switching from liquid to solid food. I recall the day I arrived home two hours late. After lunch I'd been taken to the house three doors away where friends of my parents lived who had a son of my age. I often went to Jonas, or he came to me. It was autumn, the year of the Anschluss. I wasn't allowed out in the street any more. Kroll was at Jonas's when I arrived and after tea he invited us to play in their garden across the road. There were chestnut trees, one in their ground and several abounding across walls from adjacent gardens. Seared leaves lay on the ground and chestnuts glistened from cracked skins we trod open. I'd been reminded of that garden when I'd worked at Frantelle Père et Fils, the cellar there had that dank and perfumed odour, and the calcified spiders had reminded me of that rich insect life which makes one feel an intruder in autumn gardens. Before long, hearing us play, other boys clambered over the wall and invaded the garden. They'd brought two girls along – one, I remember, with a bright scarf on her head, tied so that a red headband went across her brow. Before long the invaders started to cavort about, making war-cries by tapping their loud mouths, and chestnuts began flying about the place, the girls their targets, which made them run in zigzags to escape from being hit. After a time the chasing and running suddenly stopped, as if some referee had blown a whistle for half-time, and the intruders gathered to their half and left the three of us stranded in ours.

When it was time to resume play the girls separated from the boys and came over to us to inveigle us into joining their sport. I had no idea what was happening when the girls linked their arms into mine and coaxed me to come for a little walk. When we came to the tree they turned me round and pulled my arms to the back and round the trunk, the boys taking down the washing-lines from their posts, for that's what they used to tie me against the tree. Before long all of them, including Jonas and Kroll, were bombarding me with chestnuts. They told me afterwards they'd been threatened they'd suffer the same fate if they didn't join in.

For an endless time they went on aiming at me, all the longer as I shut my eyes to guard them from being hit, and I stood there like Samson in his weakened state trying to pull myself free, though in the process the harder I tried to pull my hands

152

free, the tighter I tied the knot holding them. And it was getting dark.

That brought sweat to my head. I had no way of telling the time and no one would talk to me. As a prisoner I was incommunicado, but I sensed it was at least an hour later than the time I should have been home. I could just about manage that if I sneaked through the kitchen door, providing our cook was in a good mood. I could stretch it by an hour any time, but more could be dangerous. I knew the rhythms of our house, the time-lags and agitations, when would those trousers I'd burnt a hole in be missed, two days and one morning, say, then questions would be asked. I was frightened that if I screamed they'd gag me. They'd threatened to. Besides, it would have added to my humiliation.

When finally they left, Kroll, our host, untied my hands and let me go. And when I got back, through the kitchen door, my mother was waiting for me and without asking me why I was late she set about beating my face with ringed hands and grabbed my shoulders when I tried to pull away, to make me take more punishment. I remember screaming at her and trying to fight my way free, but she had me in her power and neither would she listen to my excuses nor was I able under her shattering blows to get the words out. When finally she stopped she sent me to my room, and I could still hear her cursing when I slammed the door behind me and fell on the bed holding my burning head. But for my diminished strength I would gladly have killed her.

I lay for some time on the bed not knowing how to accommodate my pain and anger, and felt as tied by my frustration as I had been to that wretched tree. It must have been then that I started for the first time to wear a brown shirt and a swastika armband, elevating myself even at that tender age to the ranks of the SA. That meant I could wear jackboots to kick my mother's arse. The girl with the headband I'd made friends with as one should with an enemy, and I went about with her and sat in coffee-houses all over Vienna and took her to Grinzing to drink new wine and on our way home at night we ambushed that monster returning from some nocturnal escapade with Dr Menges, throwing her to the ground and tearing the clothes off her. We'd give her a run of terror before we kill her, we decided, and I kept up my hatred long after she'd forgotten its cause. One day I'd shoot her from the cruellest angle. I'd lie waiting for her in one of the canals near our house, my gun pointing through the grid, and I'd get my gun-moll to accost her at just the right spot so that I could put a bullet up her crutch. That was my aim, and whenever my anger wavered I'd simply touch my cheeks to remind myself how they burned that day.

But nothing happened to that corseted pig. I remember her telling Papa about what she'd done, in front of me, admonishing me once more with her sharp tongue, telling me that I should never have gone with Kroll to his garden to be attacked by that Nazi riff-raff of the neighbourhood. And all he did was to chuckle over his soup, spilling the hot liquid so that he had to hold his head back several times between spoonfuls, admiring his wife's passion. These are troubled times, he said. Tempers get frayed. The sooner we leave, the better. When he got up he stroked my cheeks.

Cruelty, Maman, took root in me with ease. Don't you believe it started there with that beating you gave me. I hope you're left with only your feelings in the ether, that your shapely and painted carcass has gone to ruin. Because I for one, God knows how many others are after you, want you to scream without being able to purse your lips for sympathy, to feel the stings when I beat you without being able to retaliate, as you no longer have hands to ward off my blows or feet to kick me with. And those umbrellas you left behind, not one of them did I bury with you in case you'd use it to gain protection in the next world, or to deflect the dangers you might encounter there.

I don't think I've ever left the world of the rebel, that insecure terrain he works in, which is never his but which he longs for, though if ever he could conquer it the first thing he'd do would be to set about its destruction. It's that tightrope existence I lead. Should I fall, whichever way, I'll end up in the wrong country. At best I observe like a spirit and play the clown, at worst I laugh in the morning and cry at night. I make excursions deep into enemy territory to sound out their intentions, I watch them betray that other country which is also me, and am on guard when they come to attack. Come, I'll show you.

This morning we were on parade, the climax of which was an inspection by Baldur von Schirach. I was in the front row and for a moment I thought he was stopping in front of me to have a few words. He looks exactly as he does in his photographs, that Austrian hero we've seen plastered on so many Viennese walls. But instead of talking to me he talked to Schmiede, that veteran Nazi next to me, who smiled as he spoke and showed that gold tooth at the front, a replacement of one he'd lost in a fight a few months ago. You look well turned out, comrade, von Schirach told him. Congratulations, *Heil Hitler!* In your honour, sir, *Heil Hitler!* Schmiede's words sped like bullets out of his mouth. The SA sergeant following the Hitler Youth leader was right in front of me, so I couldn't take a peep at Schmiede to see the pride on his face. Imagine how few of us have a chance actually to have words with our leaders. Schmiede is one of the chosen, the pride of our platoon. After the parade we drank beer in a *Keller*, and after several steins they planned their attack that night on Saalberg's the jewellers. Tell you what, said Schultz, always the ringleader when it came to Jew-bashing, we'll telephone Saalberg, that Jewish swindler, at eleven tonight and tell him his place of business is on fire. Then we smash it up, and whilst he's on his way to see the damage we'll go to his house and do that over as well. That should make him grab for his passport and beetle off. I warn Saalberg, my father knows him well, of the impending attack, and he summons forty strong Jews to stand by his shop-window that night, and six more to guard his house, and when Schultz arrives with his thugs they shout that some rat has betrayed them, and hiss abuse at those frightened Jews, and warn them they'll be back some other night.

My mother doesn't care a shit about politics, actually enjoys the danger we're in since the Anschluss, the violence in the streets and traipsing about forbidden territory. She goes on visiting the shops which have signs on their doors saying that Jews are forbidden to enter. She makes remarks, that abhorrent bitch, which come home to roost only now, that were couched in a language foreign to me at the time, to do with her cunt and nothing else about her. I do like men in uniforms, especially the cut of their trousers, and those boots which show off their legs. It suits this Hapsburg city to have soldiers swarm about the place. And men smarten up their hair and manicure their nails, uniforms inspire men to look their best. I can see her tell Mengele to keep his trousers on, just undo your flies and I'll keep my girdle on, you like that, dear, and they fuck until he has to report back for duty to dispatch a few more batches of children. God, is that why I kept on going to the enemy camps every night, to join in the destruction of Jews like her? And how did Bender find out? I remember passing him on the stairs one day, his big mouth grinning to greet me, and from sheer habit he said *Heil Hitler* instead of good day, and how I raised my hand and repeated those vile words because I was frightened not to conform. I heard him chuckle all the way up, his wife was waiting for him at the door, and I still heard their laughter when he told her what had just occurred.

And what of Alban, who ejaculated Lothar into this world? I've never mentioned this before, it's something E. should have dug up with his blunt trowel, a remark from the antiquity of my youth. A shame Papa was a Jew, Alban once told his mother, and she, that cow, passed on the remark to my father, who must have handed on that heirloom for me to remember now. Long may Alban, that impoverished ass, remember his misfortune. With my mother's nack of cruelty I've cut him out of my life, though I still have to contend with his malicious offspring.

Annie plays dreadful games with me. The other morning I had to get some pills. The doc lets me have them in small doses only, so I have to go twice a week to the surgery to be confronted by that horse-nurse who snorts at me and keeps me waiting before she produces the goodies. When I came back, Annie said Lothar had gone.

'Gone?' I asked. I should have known right from the start she was playing tricks. She smiled at my disbelief at his leaving without saying goodbye. 'Without a word?' I screamed at her, for that if nothing else confirmed my suspicions that they'd fucked together, and proved that sneak guilty.

'Yep,' she said, an expression she'd picked up from somewhere and used quite a lot lately. Then she laughed in my face.

Had Lothar really left, I worked out, she would have been sad, unless she was planning to meet up with him. I went to his room to see for myself whether his things were gone. The drawer with his shirts was empty, nothing of his was left.

'He might be back to bid you adieu,' she said. 'If not, he will telephone. You want some coffee? I've just made some fresh.'

At that moment I was so angry I could have shoved her French accent down her throat, hoping its sharp edges would saw through her vocal chords to make her speechless for ever. I went to my room and, I swear, when I came out again five minutes later to get some more coffee Lothar was there, sitting on the sofa next to Annie. I noticed he wasn't wearing any shoes, a habit he indulged in when at home, and I looked for them in the room where he'd taken them off. He said good morning to me as on any other day, and I was so bewildered by it all that I slinked towards the door of his room and opened it, to find his shoes near the bed, his clothes on several chairs, and the chest of drawers was filled with his laundry and stuff, exactly as it had been for the past three weeks.

I asked him, 'When are you off? I hear you're leaving today.

Lothar looked at Annie, sheepishly, I thought, as if to seek her protection.

'Not for another week or so unless . . .'

'Unless what?' Annie chipped in.

'You want me to go.'

'Crazy boy,' Annie said. Not only that, but she lovingly stroked his cheeks. 'I want you to stay for as long as you like, for weeks and months if you like. What is Fabrice saying? Fabrice wants Lothar to stay. Don't you, *chéri?*'

She pouted her lips in that impish way she had with those delightful red lobes of flesh, and if I'd had a tiny ball to hand I'd have stuck it into that red opening to block her seductive expression.

I'd felt quite clear that morning. The weather was fine after yesterday's rain, clear sky, you could feel the sun rise up the side of the house, and suddenly, as if clouds were cutting across that strong light, colours faded as did shadows, and my muzzy brain let in confusion. I'm used to seeing things, and can tell hallucination from what I see, I've been there before. But I'm not used to tricks. It's nasty to go to the length of emptying a room, to make me go in and see, then filling it up again as if nothing had been moved. Downright nasty, that is. And then to tell me what I longed to hear, that Lothar was at last going to leave me in peace, and then deny that what I'd so clearly heard had been said at all, the two of them enacting some game to drive me crazy, to get me into a bin and out of the way! Thank God I felt suddenly so drained I wanted to lie down and sleep. I felt tired as when some nights I wake like a drunkard to pee. If I'd had the strength I'd have gone for that gun to shoot that monstrous pair goading me to madness.

'Of course,' I said, 'do stay as long as you like.'

I wanted to add that perhaps I'd misunderstood. I hadn't, but I did not dare state that possibility in case I'd make them think they'd succeeded in confusing me. I went to my room and left them to their sniggering and talking behind my back.

That evening rain fell over London. The day had turned sultry, heat was like fever in the air, you were loath to breathe near the patient in case you caught the disease. I've spent much time looking out of my window, there's always so much to see, yet, strangely enough, little to remember. I think it is because the trees and shrubs are constantly changing, and though their daily growth is imperceptible our expectation of growth is not, and we see what we look for or think we see what we seek. That makes us keep on looking for wondrous things. In summer the trees rise to the height of my window, but not near enough for

158

me to touch the leaves, and that day, probably on account of my lonely condition, that's what I wanted to do, to extend my world to find safety. I aimed carefully as I threw several books from my second-floor window on to the lawn for a soft landing, then most of my clothes, including the shirts I'd brought from Africa, some still in their wrappings. They swished nicely through the air and zigzagged and crashed like paper planes out of balance. And all kinds of other items I wanted to use for the garden party, a box of candles I'd bought when a fuse bust one day, and spare hangers from my cupboard for the shoulders of my guests. Then I went down and slipped past the side of Frau Eppstein's flat into the garden, and spread my suit and shirts over the shrubs.

It was wet and still raining outside, a boon to my efforts, as my clothes were more easily shaped to sit or recline, to be grouped so that my guests could mingle, and for females to use my shirts for skirts. The candles, alas, because of the rain, were useless. Old Archer arrived with Miss Lampert and they started to dance, humming old tunes from the twenties when they were young, and certain selected windows opened and people began joining the singing, gently at first, taking time to retrieve their memories – when had they last heard these songs? Their bodies ached less as they spanned the distance to when they'd danced to those tunes, their flesh was suddenly supple, you could see them sway at their windows, dancing and humming and singing. The neighbourhood was alive and, my God, what had I started, they wouldn't stop their singing and dancing – as if they were to cease, they'd never dance again. We simply had to have light to stop people falling and bumping into each other, and I found that the books were dry enough to burn, and once I got them alight in a heap I stuck candles round the perimeter of the pyre, which soon started to burn because the heat of the fire was soaking up the rain. When the fire was roaring I took all the clothes I could find and burned them too, for now I wanted everyone to play naked in the rain and dance in bare feet on the lawn. That was nice.

Poor boy, I heard Frau Eppstein say as they brought me back

159

indoors late at night, shivering. It had turned cold. I'd snuggled up to the dying embers of the fire, but the fire was dead when they found me asleep in the garden.

I was tired the next day, so terribly tired, and cold through and through. Then the fever died down. Oh, how I enjoy recovering, but Lothar was still there and spoiled it for me. I love those shines I get when I get well after some bout of illness, cajoling my senses to feel once more what I can best describe as purity, that point of feeling we're at which is the result of the benign history of our perceptions after the twisting flashes and dreams which make us wake as heavy as lead – oh, those terrible bugs which attack my head and make me feel hollow, totally hollow, so I feel I have no organs left inside me. No doubt my desire to work at Frantelle Père at Fils had at the time to do with the pleasure I envisaged each day of emerging from dark cellars, to see once again light and colours, to hear unechoing voices instead of whispers in the dark, as if those casks had held corpses awaiting burial.

But Lothar was there. Every time I reached for Annie he put his hand across my eyes and shut her out. Whenever she came to my room he followed her, or he stood outside my cell with his bunch of keys. I knew it was him at the door-handle, since because of his gammy leg his balance faltered when he came to the door and for a second or two he leaned on the handle, then stood back to open up. And in she walked, holding a tray with food, and chirped perfunctory sentences at me. Zee vezzer is cold outside. I go shopping now, you be all right for an hour, yes? *Lotharre* will stay behind.

To tell her to take that fucker with her might have given away how much I'd really recovered, and I wanted my recovery to be slow and good, a real piece of physical craftsmanship so that I could write once more, this time the best poetry in England.

Another reason for my wishing for a slow recovery was my fear of never finishing what I set out to do, and thus I wanted to delay my start. I thought I'd struck a rich seam when I decided, as soon as I was well again, to write exactly about how I worked, thus to exorcise that crippling fault in me which always prevents me from fulfilling the promise of my opening lines. To plan a poem, that spark of heaven which comes to light your eyes, like that unattainable woman in the crowd who suddenly comes towards you to be yours or to make you hers, that marvellous coming together when words flow like inspiration and our greedy love makes us into new beings which, later on, we graft on our past with our arms open to receive the future together, oh how, tell me, can I separate my art from my life? All the Lothars of my life keep putting their cold hands over my eyes, they spoil my vision and paralyse my feet. I can't run away from this bondage, my body simply won't carry me beyond that intersection where the culled nectar of my life lies cupped, and the forces beyond make me go berserk. I turn Annie from the good to the evil virgin of my cathedral door, have toads and worms creep up her and insects to disfigure her skin. I search for abhorrence on her which will make me turn away from her, but find only, when I steal a glance at her, that beauty I saw in the colonnade when I first spotted her. I'm sick of my love for her and hope she loves Lothar well, with a passion not dissimilar to mine, so I can make her scream for years when I snort him out of existence. For I don't really see why I alone should suffer because Annie wants to change horses. If I can't make her feed me with her love in return for mine, I'll wipe out Lothar to make her suffer like me. That's only fair.

The next day I woke up reborn and full of energy, the way Annie likes me. My skin felt better, inside and out, it's a feeling I get when my flesh is the right temperature and my hair has shine and my vision is sharp. A few endearments from Annie, some sign that she's watching me, and my anguish melts. We went for a picnic in the park, the three of us, and I remember we talked of ordinary things, told anecdotes from our lives we'd not told before, and we'd have played with a beach-ball after lunch if we'd had one, but instead we picked some long blades of grass and Lothar taught us how to hold them like reeds between our thumbs and blow shrill notes.

A few languid days followed, days of quiet and pleasant

living, with holiday tempers I remembered from when Papa was still alive spent on the African shore, the incoming tides mesmerizing me with the incoming water monotonous in its approach, and the tingling terror I felt when Maman kept warning us as the tide was ebbing to take care not to be dragged out to sea. The receding tide is as dangerous as a snake. But at the back of my mind, no matter how far I wandered into the past to call up what knowledge I possessed, lay that dog Lothar at the door of my house, basking in the sun until you got to within two feet of him, when he started to growl and rattle with violence. The only way to get in was to shoot him first. And that, believe me, was frightening, the fact that no matter how I tried to secure my life, I felt I was drifting towards killing that dog. I'll not eat meat for a week to see whether that will help. I'll visit the elevated parts of London so as to get away from the flat surface of Earls Court, because I feel I am stuck yet drifting out to sea. Maman was right about so many things. How did that Austrian yodeller know about the sea? When the tide changes and the waves come in once more they'll carry me to land all right. Until then, hold on and keep your power dry.

Sixteen

Listen to the drums! It's been going on for four days, some kids in the street, and I thought it'd be all over after the street festival which took place two days ago. They've kept the drums strapped round their waists; all day and all night they keep up their beat. It's astonishing no one has complained. Annie says it's on account of the pigeons which have descended over the neighbourhood. They foul up the parapets and spoil our gardens, and the drums stop the birds from alighting, so either they'll move on or drop exhausted to the ground and starve to death. I've not been out of the house because I can't bear to see dead creatures. When the drumming stops, the noise will go on for days in my ears.

I've been listening to my heartbeats and wonder whether we don't always listen for these. It's our innermost sound we take for granted, but at times, as when those drumbeats led me to listen, we dare ourselves to wait for the missing beat and smile at our survival. At times I feel nothing whatever is wrong with my life. Schloss keeps sending me money, Annie is as sweet as a ripe peach, not a fruit I choose at random to describe her, but because there's the softest hair at the small of her back and rising up the inside of her thighs, and Lothar is a charming guest to have around, he's content with everything we do and admires our life-style, Annie's French cuisine and my grappling with words and mixing with the poets of England. We have fine, clear days between us. I feel secure because life is flowing and I don't see an end anywhere to my flotation; it's the middle of a thousand leagues of blue, nowhere in sight of land where all hurt takes place. Here there are millions of mixed shades and shadows, drowned dreams, somnambulism, reveries, all that we call lives and souls lie dreaming, dreaming, still; tossing the slumberers in their beds, the ever-rolling waves but made so by their restlessness. Until, that is, clouds appear and blacken the sky, precursors of the winds which come raging at us to punish us for those few hours we felt significant. You've stolen some peace and the wind has been sent after us to lash us back to land. And there, once more, I tremble.

They laugh at me for trembling. It's true I cannot hold still. The liquid in my glass almost spills over, and I laugh too easily and am eager to be heard when I speak. Thus I make gestures with my head, it comes from having an agile body, I'm fit and haven't put on any weight for the past fifteen years. And I'm tall, nearly six feet, the depth of a grave, and I'm conscious of my feet. I've never broken a bone, a sign that I tread carefully upon the ground. I'm not happy the way my arms hang from my shoulders. There's too much dangling, my thumbs curve to the right and left of me, they should point to the front and I make them do so but that, over the years, has given me somewhat rounded shoulders, a stance my mother constantly objected to. Stand up straight, Fabrice, or you'll topple over. Her back was straight all right, she had little choice in the matter with her tight corsets, and I always objected to her objection about the way I held myself, but lately I have taken note of what she said and correct my poise when I become aware of how badly I stand. There's a little muscular pain I feel when I relax too long, and I then brace myself, with excellent results. Annie, when she notices, praises me and tells me how handsome I now look, tall and strong. I get her to bed simply by standing up straight. As for my face, I know it only from the front - even less, that is, than the rest of my body. I often play with the molars on the left, grinding the upper and lower together, sometimes the right ones too, which makes my mouth mobile even when I'm not using it for some practical purpose, and this has given me the idea ever since I can remember that my teeth, through my constantly flexing them, are tough enough to chew piano-strings. I have strong curly hair which Annie cuts for me every fortnight or so, and as my locks fall on the towel she's draped around my shoulders she keeps telling me I'm the envy of girls with such beautiful hair. There's grey appearing amidst the brown, but I don't ever see that on my head in the mirror, only in the tufts Annie has cut. I drag my little finger across the page when I write. It's in the way, I don't quite know what to do with it.

They're still beating their drums, or are they? The noise is too loud for lingering echoes. Drum-rolls roll, then fade, it seems nothing whatever stays at the same pitch, and some leaders of the band revive the beats with such energy you think they'll never stop. Perhaps by tonight it'll be all over, and they'll dispose of the dead pigeons. Old Archer will pluck a few feathers for his nest. He'll use one to tickle Miss Lampert's erogenous spots or as a quill to write her name upon his heart.

I've not seen Marie-Claire or Chaim for some time, and this is simply to say that I remember them well but that I've had no particular wish to see them.

Somehow, ever since the first sputnik rocketed into space, Annie and I have depopulated our world and roamed alone through space, though lately we've been strapped in with that dog Lothar as our travelling companion. When our mission is accomplished we'll land and go our separate ways. What a relief after such proximity! I'll go back to the houses I lived in, Vienna, Jo'burg, Paris and London, and find strangers have lived there, nothing looks quite the same. There's nothing here I wish to call my own, not even my desk with its barely visible layer of dust over everything. I wipe it clean with my hand, some pages of unfinished stuff, I read a few lines and vaguely remember I wrote them, and the distant mood which made me write them down. It's time, I feel, to move on, after travelling round the world several times it's hard to stay in one place, though Annie humming to herself immediately sets about cleaning up and making our flat shipshape. ''ere we are,' she calls out in a loud voice. I like her melodious voice when she uses it full blast: '*Chéri, Lotharre*, coffee!' She puts the tray down on the table, and we appear to wet our whistles and plan the afternoon. Annie wants us to take a boat on the Thames and steam to Greenwich. It's a nice day for it, sun and little wind, but I don't feel like being confined on deck, not so soon after our space flight, and I tell them I must stay behind to write a report for the CIA, which perhaps I shouldn't have mentioned because it made Lothar and Annie look at one another in a peculiar way. Not that I meant the CIA in Washington, DC. I work for one which is controlled by Madame Parapluie, wherever she is.

There's so much to report, Madame, above all about the aching heart. Friend and foe have taken up positions, the latter is heavily armed, I suspect there'll be a pre-emptive strike and that there's no time left for diplomatic discussions. Two years ago they started firing missiles at each other, flowers and poems at first, and marvellous revelations which exploded in the middle of their lives, but lately they've used some dangerous ammunition, there've been one or two fatal hits, and now both sides are getting angry. You remember (see previous reports) how at the beginning Annie had to hide me from that one-armed bandit and his consort to keep her allowance intact, when we came to Paris whilst she was still supposed to be studying at that Berlitz school in London? I had no idea at the time, I wasn't paying attention, but in fact she was an expert at hiding things. Later on she once told me of her early training, how she used to put little parcels of food under the arched root of a tree, or underneath stones, for those creatures she'd talked to in the country gardens she visited on outings with her parents, hoping thereby to abate the anger of magicians who'd rise up when two dewdrops touched to fulfil some wish of hers, or at least let her watch their splendid acts. How did I not notice these subtle touches of privacy which later on caused me such anguish when I read them as deviousness? It's not that she took on lovers behind my back, but that she kept part of her world intact by not allowing me to share in it, as if not wishing to risk everything with me, keeping escape routes free so that, if she ran away, I'd never find her. Like that fellow Jaulin, on whom I never set eyes, working from some remote address, or those friends from the USA who'd invited her to dine at La Perouse but didn't turn up on account of their drug-sucking son, whereupon she rang me via Sabatine and I picked her up in her Parisian chic and took her on a pleasure-boat down the Seine. Having prepared herself all day for her exclusive evening, and planned the day before what to wear, she was glad enough to be rescued by me – I was good enough for that, but not for meeting her friends. And I cursed myself at the time, and for some days afterwards, for eating my pride, never a good repast, and humbling myself to save her from a sordid exit from that posh restaurant.

Other cracks I now perceive, hair-thin at first, over the months and years they've widened into gaping cuts which will in time cause the fabric of our love to collapse. She cursed me one day and let fly: oh, you and your work, it's far more important to eat! That's what she said, *ma petite bourgeoise*, that venomous curse has left a scar and I've not trusted her since. She'd felt so cold and hungry that day, she said, it had made her demented. If that were true, then why, on another occasion, did she say she'd love me just as well were I not a poet, the man comes first and after that his art? That's never been my sequence. She diminishes me by her stupidity, but then what do you expect from a Frog, which gets its kicks from catching flies and shedding its sperm in water? Sometimes when I touch Annie in bed, when her sensitive zones evade my arousal and she takes ages to respond, I reverse my bedtime story and turn my princess back into a frog, let sleeping frogs lie, as it were, withhold magic from this amphibious creature. I fall asleep next to her, find enough space in our bed to be out of touch, and an hour later I'm woken by her gentle croaking and with one touch she becomes transformed again into that enchanting woman I love so much. But one day my touch will fail me, I know, and my investment in her company won't be worth a sou. We might as well call a creditors' meeting right away and prepare ourselves for the event.

As Managing Director of the bankrupt company Annie chairs the meeting, a subtle rule at such proceedings. Her role is to explain her failure to her creditors. I'm so sorry you 'ave lost your money, I 'ave no idea where the cash leaked out, why, in fact, the business failed. I think our problem was overtrading, too much was demanded of us, it's 'ard to stop the momentum of sales once you've started. She starts off like that, her voice at its best, firm and clear, with just a slight tremor at the back so as not to sound entirely fearless, which could be interpreted as arrogance. She's going to give a good performance all right, though none of the creditors will leave with any hope of getting their money back. I invested everything I 'ad in the company, my 'air, my nose, my eyes and my busoms. She lists every part of herself including her cunt, stretching her investment as far as she possibly can. I sit there as her biggest creditor by far and take note of her assets before I start asking one or two questions. I'm not her only creditor; others are present as well. There's never only one when it comes to failure. Zee business of love is very complicated, she says, we thought we 'ad it right, Fabrice and I spotting each other in the rain and falling 'ead over 'eels in lurve. Now she's really pushing her accent, and she sounds fishy when she talks like that. I 'ad no idea, and nobody warned me, that I vos going to live viz *un homme si difficile*, 'e was so amusing but also so frightening at times, it brings blotches to my skin if I'm frightened all day and night. But don't be frightened by 'im. I 'ave got to know 'im so well, 'e's gentle and warm as fur, 'e'll never 'arm anyone except 'imself sometimes when 'e goes wild and bangs 'is 'ead against the wall, when 'e acts like a . . . ram on 'eat.

I love hearing her grope for images, at times they get twisted by two languages bending the metal and come out a hilarious mishmash. It's hard to sustain anger, and as she goes on I completely forget the questions I wanted to put to her, at hearing her voice they recede like a snail's horns and disappear

168

inside my head.

And so it was with her other creditors. Maman earlier had made an unruly interruption. How dare you take away your love from Fabrice? When you came along I handed him over to you. Am I now to take back that young monkey? Everyone laughed at her for having made a monkey of herself by her droll admonishment. I 'ad no idea, Madame Parapluie, I vos competing viz you! With that Annie made a gesture with her hand that tore Maman's umbrella to shreds, and all that Maman could do was to join in the laughter, which endeared her to us all.

Lothar had come too, but had sat at the back, an observer to watch what was going on and also, as the new man in Annie's life, to act as her protector. I felt his stare touch me. I thought of a rainbow spanning from Annie to him, that's what it was, why the light at odd moments was spectrum bright. They sent messages to each other on every colour and shade and their combined power made her send everyone off with *une puce à l'oreille*, that's what she meant, the dear chic, though she said, 'I vont you to flee viz your ears!'

All this gets me nowhere, my attempt to put fear on paper won't stop the hounds in my blood from pursuing that stuffed hare and I'm left holding my betting-slip until the race is over and I lose far more than I win. I'm besotted with tension, the excitement of the race doesn't diminish because the hare is false, the dogs won't ever get their paws on it and gut it with relish. And below tension lies fear, I see its monstrous claws everywhere, ready to pounce and tear my peace apart.

And let me tell you what above all frightens me, *chère Madame*. Through some restlessness which, I suspect, entered me through your twitching womb, I can't get rid of the image that has haunted me over the years, ever since I made it with women, of you looking over Papa's shoulders for the next and better opportunity. I've often left and have often returned. Change occurs, so many changes I cannot get used to them, there's never enough time to make for permanence before I leave again. I lead the life of a fledgling the mother bird turns from her nest, and fledgling I remain, like a sailor who looks to sea or land, yearning simply to journey forth and never to remain. It's best described, this turbulent malaise, this rolling life, in unfixed terms, myself the stone in that river at the Val des Cousins, beneath the polishing, clear water, the gargoyle embraced by Quasimodo's loving arm, stones have so much time I envy them, that's where longing lies, the faster I move the more my longing surges up in me, my light flotsam body has nothing to hold on to, the brain can't cope with that longing. I drift on the current of the sea or on trade winds until the monsoon in my head strikes and makes my light go out. Hear me, Maman, sit still and listen. When the pain strikes I am dislodged, nothing then matters except to end this pain; for hours I find no position to lay my head, I become like an animal writhing in pain, the goats Lothar shot on Kramer's farm, all he wanted, my amorous successor, was a witness to their suffering. I want you to feel my pain, Maman, and share a little of it. That's all I ask. No further help is needed.

Ha, I've got her frightened. That cold winging in the air is her, that monstrous bat has fused umbrellas to her arms and bangs her head in daylight. I'll chase her to the brightest place I know and watch her whimpering decline in hell. Or no, just before she reaches the blinding heat which will singe her wings I'll put out the flames and make her see in the dark. She'll settle on some rafter in my head - watch out, they'll say, he's batty. Before long they'll come once more for me, to take me away. But I'll not tell them what's gone on in my head, I won't tell anyone, they'll never find Fabrice.

Seventeen

Book Five. I know what to do, the thrust of the samurai's sword, one swing he's practised all these years, there's no tolerance for error, off comes the enemy's head. The victim, poor fellow, is not tied down, he's not strapped to the post with his prick upstanding, his eyeballs and tongue ready to pop out the moment he swings. Nor will the executioner tolerate defiance, allowing the prisoner to poke his tongue out at him. He'd have him whipped to teach him one final lesson before releasing the trap. There is no simple execution according to law. Nevertheless, though parallel lines never meet, there are similarities in direction.

The thing to do, first of all, is to keep your anger alive. That's a tough discipline, for I'm used to pendulum thoughts, but here no contrasts are allowed, no slack swing to see what it looks like the other side. I wish, for example, that Lothar would not remove the itch on his cheek with his finger, I wish he'd hold still for a moment with one eye half closed to reveal how alive he is that even the weight of an eyelash can cause discomfort. Or when he talks to me, not knowing what's to come. He chases me back to that kinship I felt the first time I met him in Vienna, he was on my side then all right, I assure you, and now we face one another, he my enemy. I've gone beyond doubt about him and Annie, there's no question he's left his mark on her, I can't get his dirt off her delicate texture, the colour is fading on the spots I rub; before long there'll be nothing but holes and I'll

171

have to discard her.

I've walked, lately, all over London to dispel the curse of that gun. It draws me, that lethal weapon, a powerful magnet far beyond its metal. I think by the time I get to Kennington across the river I'll attain a distance where its force weakens, but that's not so and by the time I reach Clapham Common I know that distance from the drawer at Earls Court where Lothar's gun lies wrapped in his shirt does not cure me of my intent. I keep walking simply to occupy myself, to engage my mind and to compose a few lines. Now and again I stop to jot them down. But like some orbiting evil, however my head is occupied at the time, Annie the Devil spots me where I stand, and tells me all is lost and that our love is over. *Verweile doch, du bist so schön.* It's no use, this one-sided pleading. She's like a season come to an end. The harvest, such that it is, lies gathered in the barn.

Maman always wanted me to have style. *Style* is so important, she used to blabber, it doesn't matter what a man does as long as he has *style*. It depends, of course, on what you consider to be style. The sharp crease in his trousers, his standing up when she entered the room and kissing her hand, smelling her perfume and touching her polished nails. Josef Mengele's style was enough for her to forgive his little misdemeanours. It's quite ridiculous, she used to say, to be righteous in a world so full of injustice, you haven't the chance to put everything to rights, so you might as well have a good time and enjoy yourself to the brim. Mind you, she expected you to be qualified for life, quick-witted and smart, cunning, sly, amusing and, I fondly remember above all, if you can make people laugh you'll be a wow. In addition, if you had money that'd be no hindrance, there's so much pleasure to buy, she used to say, I can happily spend a fortune every day. She used to make her bodyguard of pets stand upright, standing up straight was part of style, no crippled backs, for God's sake, or gammy legs. Stand up straight, my pet, she used to say to me, her chief pet, and Louise too was made to deport herself properly; I don't mind how much you swing your behind but your back's got to be straight. That's beautiful, she used to praise her when she carried a tray and looked an L to the waist.

So now, what would you have me do for style, Madame Parapluie? Put my life at risk and fight a duel with Lothar? You know I'm not an early riser at the best of times, and I'd arrive an hour late at the appointed place with a sour taste in my mouth, so unpleasant I couldn't shoot straight. Then just shoot, my pet, simply choose a good moment and shoot and don't aim at the face, it makes an awful mess. Any time is a good time to get rid of a rival, do it in the afternoon, late afternoon is best, the time they kill bulls in Spain. Nothing seems too cold-blooded at that time of day, there's the whole night in front of you to get over the shock and consternation you'll arouse, women can weep without being seen properly and men can drown their agitation in drink. Between five and when the evening star appears is best, the witch advises. She has beguiling power, particularly now she dwells in twilight. In Africa she kept the curtains drawn all day, it kept the house cool and her mind in a state in which at any time she could pounce into the light simply by lifting the curtain hiding her confessor, to lead him into temptations and sins she'd just described. I'll have nothing said against her amoral existence, I tolerate her the same as I do Santa Teresa who asks us to believe that her heart was pierced by a spear of divine love. That word divine, my Lord, has gone out of existence, it went kaput at Auschwitz, and all that's left is imperfection.

I'm about to have pain, perhaps in fourteen days. I know the timetable, exactly when pain passes through tunnels hundreds of miles away, crosses mountains and shifts through green valleys, draws nearer all the time until it reaches the station in my head. When it gets to London the ache in my heart will be so severe that sex will be drained from my loins and Annie will ask frightening questions. Are you all right, my pet? She culls my mother's words from the twlight in my ears, I choke in her grip and fight myself free from her embrace. Tears flow down my cheek. Pain has no hand-grip in its ghostly wagons, there's nowhere to hold on to, it stops nowhere for the traveller to get some refreshment or to wipe the grime off his face after a

173

long journey. Whatever view I take of Lothar, whatever medication he may administer to tone down my shriek, I know the pumping in my head will soon be so loud that I shan't be able to hear him, and the pain will make me misread his lips when he pleads for mercy.

But before I strike, before the final blow, let me empty my house. It is always best, we are told, to look at the future, and we've followed that instruction since time immemorial and have written heaven and hell into our scriptures. I've tried so often to empty my house of the rubbish I've gathered, to make a fresh start. That's why I've so seldom finished what I wanted to say, new ideas catch up on the old to lap them up before they themselves are overtaken. I wonder what remains today of the toys we left in Vienna, whether some child since grown into a man has handed on to his children some pieces blemished by knocks but durable beyond the flesh? I'll finally get rid of the dust in the crevices of distant memory, and whilst we're rummaging in the attic where they stored our pram and rattles – we had no more children, my mother once said, 'for political reasons', two was enough to cope with in those troubled times – we might as well move on to that Paris mansard and clear out what remains of those happy times with Annie. Avoid, new lover in my erstwhile nest, that creaking floor-board when you get up at night to pee so as not to wake your slumbering love, and give Sabatine all the things we left behind, including that pot of *confiture de cerises* I bought at Fourchamps, one of the extravagances we never got round to eating. And wipe our dust away. And Mother's clothes, with their frightening power stuck in my head, they too must go. I'll break that bondage now and stop that mimicry. I've never told anyone how I used to dress, putting my socks on I pulled my stockings high, reversed my pants to have no slit in front, girdled my midriff by pulling my belt tight, all those tricks towards nearness with her clothes I played, though not once did I deprave my maleness by trespassing into her ways, step into her clothes when no one was looking or paint my face, but now my wings are tired and treading air no longer pleases me.

174

In the end I'll also spew out the vocabulary in my head. I've done with words. They lace me to meaning which changes and I'm left with hollow sounds and wounding memories. I love you, she said, and now she protests that her feelings are unchanged, but there's been movement and shift, and love, that star word in our life, has become worn and twisted with use, it has withered into common parlance and I might as well throw it out. And in any case why, I ask myself, must my head be cluttered up with *aides-mémoires*, words that cling like urchins to my skull, they wink and lift their skirts like whores offering to trade their use for memories I simply don't wish to recall? Someone will give me food and water without words when I ask for it, and succour as to a traveller in remote lands. I'll use my hands more, and my tongue to lick and chew, and my lips to kiss and laugh.

So there!

He sits there, that idiot enemy of mine, Lothar. I've got the gun, have had it for two days now and he's not noticed it's missing from the drawer. I had assumed he was more cunning than that. I'd have thought he'd miss that hard object rolled into his shirt, that he'd keep in touch with it as I do with Bonzo, however far away he squats, the old dear. I'm more the animal than Lothar is, my purpose more direct. I sniff the trails of my desires whilst he moves in more complicated ways, so much so that he's constantly distracted and easy to waylay. He will keep walking about the house in his socks, a fact which greatly disturbs me. Shoes cover a nakedness concerned with innocence which I don't wish to see at present. When the fellow is dead he'll be wearing his own stiff hide, but until then his flesh is soft and I want him garbed in his shoes and clothes. That way my hatred is geared. I'll catch him before he goes on his daily jaunt with Annie; he always waits on the sofa all ready to go whilst she puts the final touches to her face. She'll scream the house down, that'll be fun to witness. Whom will she cry out for, him or me? Most likely, after a minute's wailing, for herself, for her ensuing loneliness after the drama is over, after the fuzz have come to haul me off, for I've no intention at present of running away. Should I, by the time I pull the trigger, think of an escape route, I'll certainly follow it, but I doubt whether at this late stage one will come to mind. I've often thought of where to go, how to escape and by what route, but there's nowhere left to go where I'd feel safe. I'll keep on thinking, I've not yet given up all hope for safety.

Eighteen

Whilst I've been waiting for my coup marvellous clarity has come to my head. I feel light and nimble, there's no ache anywhere in my body, my mind's made up, and my will is my command. My surroundings have become confined, I don't look out of my window any more. I hardly venture outside, and when I do I notice my eye has stopped roving, such is my pleasure at concentrating on what's about to happen that I have no interest in anything else, though I've written some poems these past few days, quite a number. Perhaps my decision to get rid of words has caused some consternation in my head, with words fighting each other to get used one more, a charming thought which I fouled up in one of the poems by recalling Jews jumping the queues to the showers at Auschwitz. Thus were they teased to their extermination.

Annie has noticed my changed mood and likes me the better for it. There's a craving in women which seeks an object for sympathy, and my waning libido these last fourteen days has enlivened her curiosity no end. You 'ave been viz another woman, you naughty boy, she says when I turn away from her at night after she's displayed herself as best she can. Oh, what passion she aroused in me when I looked through all the keyholes of her life as she lay in my arms after the rub of love! But now she's my target for punishment. I'm careful not to forgive her, the temptation is there more often than I care to admit, but that's yet another meaning of keeping your powder dry, don't let sentiments blur the image if you want to shoot straight. And I too have talks with myself when I speak against my will. Go off course. It'll bring disaster to you all. With Annie's plaints calling up Frau Eppstein, and Heidi in Vienna screaming her head off for her lost son, can you imagine what noise there will be? And the police rough-handling me, I'll scream blue murder when they grip my arms to arrest me, and that ride when I'll sit manacled to those strangers, what will that do to Marie-Claire, to Colette and Claire and those corseted friends of my mother's who've lived in my head all these years, who've strapped me down to administer their ways on me? You'll be glad to be shot of them, my will answers back, and that is right. I'm sick of the crowd in my head, I seek a solution. Perhaps, though, my surging flow of work is caused simply because of my studied avoidance of Lothar. He respects what I do and would never come to my room unless I asked him to, and this I certainly wouldn't do. So I'm forced for once to sit at my desk with a stern master at my back who keeps me on course and doesn't allow me time even between poems in case that gap should allow my new-found discipline to ebb away. Or else I'm racing away because there's little time left, the end of life is in sight and you'd better get something done before it's too late. But that's not how I feel. I have endless time left.

Tomorrow is Thursday, named after the god of thunder, a good day for firing a gun. Yesterday Annie came to my room for a chat. I detested her interrogation, her subtle and clever questions as to the why of my strange behaviour. 'We 'ave got to 'ave a talk, you and I,' she said after she'd knocked at my door and I'd let her in. She stood there, I could see she wouldn't sit down until I asked her to, which I did. 'I'm frightened, I don't know why. It's exactly because I don't know vot's the matter that I'm afraid. If you won't tell me, then I'll go away. At once. It's not fair that you treat me like ziss. Vot's going on in your 'ead? Are you not well? Is it me, is it *Lotharre?* There's nothing but air left between us, I might as well not be 'ere. You 'ave thrown me out but 'aven't told me to go!'

I should have got up and gone over to her to put my arms

around her. But that's not what my will commanded, and for that moment, thank God, it was stronger than my inclination. Also it forced me to lie.

'I'm absorbed in my work at present, I've no head for anything else. For years I've waited for poems to pour out of me. It happens to poets. After long fallow periods there are suddenly a lot of poems. Please understand.'

That half-lie worked wonders on her. The stress on her face seemed suddenly to disperse, the bitch didn't even ask what I'd written – something, quite frankly, I'd foreseen, else I'd not have used this lie for an excuse, for in my poems she might have detected clues to my forthcoming deed, and those I had to hide at all costs.

'When, *chéri*, will you be nice to me again – you know, make lurve? I miss you so much! It's been ages since you touched me. I cannot live under one roof with a stranger.'

'Friday,' I said. 'That's not long to wait? Or tonight, if you'd like.' I wanted to say just after lunch tomorrow, before I shoot Lothar. Matadors make love before a corrida, there's fondness and farewell in the act, and it calms their nerves. She was pleased, so much so that she forgave me my lack of spontaneous desire. I don't think she saw any signs of danger, though I'm sure she wasn't her old self for the rest of the day. Nothing but penetration would do the trick. She came over and kissed me before she left, an adieu till that night. And then she stroked the back of my head. That was nice.

I'd decided, when Lothar and Annie were out that afternoon, as I'd never used a revolver in my life, to fire one practice shot. Sometimes Annie forgets something, so I waited for forty minutes exactly after they'd gone before taking the gun from the pocket of one of my suits hanging in the wardrobe. It had occurred to me that it was providential that Lothar had brought the weapon which would kill him. I'd read, over the years, stories in newspapers, snippets I'd kept in my mind, of men purchasing their own coffins before they died, lying in them to try them out for size, one man, I remember, insisting that the undertaker screw down the lid and leave him there for two full days and nights so that he'd get used to the dark. And somehow I linked Lothar's portage of his gun to his managing his affairs to the very end, providing, if he had to die, even the weapon that would kill him. A pretty thought, Bonzo agreed. And the more careful you've got to be, Bonzo warned, because in that case he'll expect to be shot. I practised handling the gun, putting my index finger on the trigger inside my coat pocket before I pulled out the gun, so that with one move I was ready to shoot. There'd be no time for Lothar to wriggle out of line, his gammy leg strapped him to the chair.

When I had finished practising, a forty-five-minute lesson I gave myself, I got up from the chair I'd be sitting in tomorrow and moved it an inch or two, making perfect the alignment with my target. I licked my lips, they dry up when I get excited, I felt saliva exude from the corners of my mouth, that extra salivation I connect with the hangman's ecstasy as he prepares the gallows for his victim. I'd have used my hand to wipe my mouth, but having held a deadly weapon in it I used my arm instead to avoid contamination.

I had a marvellous time that night. Annie and Lothar came back late that afternoon and, to celebrate the prospects of the night, Annie had bought lobsters for supper. They're for *Lotharre*, she said. I lurve them too, she added, to ameliorate her lie, they're a great delicacy in Vienna, he tells me. There's no sea in Austria. She laughed. I detected mockery about a country with no sea. I could hear her whisk the mayonnaise in the kitchen whilst I had a snifter with our guest. The whole evening I kept him amused so as to prevent him from visiting his room. I was afraid some late resurgence of his cunning might tell him the gun was missing. There'd already been one hiccup, when he removed his shoes and got up to take them to his room. I held back from offering to do this for him so as not to arouse suspicion, and I was still wiping the cold sweat from my brow when he returned. I don't know why, perhaps because this was to be our last conversation, more likely though because I expect resolutions to rise up when the time and place are opportune to make drifting strands coalesce, I expected Lothar to startle me

180

about his means. That had always been a puzzle to me. When he came back he told me, without prompting, what I had wanted to know.

'I've written to them and told them not to send any more money.'

That's what he said as he sat down and picked up his glass. The tone of his voice implied that I knew whom he was talking about, and though my suspicion was right I must have looked somewhat perplexed.

'Kramer,' he said. 'I blackmailed him. I had evidence from my father that he'd worked with Mengele in the experimental block at Auschwitz and I used it to get cash for myself. Nice fat sums I received from some bank in Paraguay. "Instead of using animals to test drugs for human beings, we used human beings to test drugs for animals." That's what he wrote to me when he agreed to pay. Some apologia! "I consider animals to be the more important of the two." What a number, that thug. That's why I shot his goats instead of him.'

I had my suspicions all along, had even thought exactly along the lines Lothar had just confessed. Nevertheless I was shocked, and then enraged by that scoundrel opposite me, that Viennese ponce.

'Does Annie know?' I asked.

'No, and please don't tell her,' he pleaded.

'I shan't.'

That, quite frankly, was my will talking. Don't be a fool, don't diminish him in her eyes so as to lessen her punishment tomorrow afternoon. Furthermore, I was determined not to think about him any longer, the outline of my target was fixed in my mind and I wanted no pollution of my object. And I left his confession at that and talked no further about it. Instead I described the sea to him, and how lobsters shed their shell as they grow.

I wanted time to pass quickly that night. I had good reason, and for several minutes when I didn't have to perform to keep Lothar amused, Annie having come in for a sherry which she sipped next to him, I imagined myself to be in charge of time, lopping a minute or two off every hour in London – oh, the grumbles and screams I heard from children having to go to bed a little early, of husbands refusing their food as, after a few days of shrinking time, they'd only just eaten an hour or so before they came home for their evening meal, and bells ringing time, you were suddenly conscious of how many clocks there were, and before long the ringing of bells was continuous, and the preacher's sermon unending, there was unbelievable chaos everywhere with foreigners, whose time I'd not interfered with, arriving with apparent delays, their appointments and schedules gone for a burton, and that would ensue until I'd fired my shot, when everything would return to normal.

I flummox time whenever I can. I am not, remember, regular, a fact my mother disapproved of so much that she threatened Louise with beatings several times if she found no way to train me. I was happy that night, the weight of listening to what Lothar and Annie were saying to each other, those notes I'd heard over the past few weeks which made me compose tunes of a thousand jealousies, this weight had lifted and I was free once more to listen to the buzzing fly enraged by the transparent window-pane, a buzz I readily transferred to my head in order to inspire groping thoughts to come to light. When you are happy, time passes quickly and you long for more.

Ah, the way Annie laid the table and prepared the food was festive. She'd bought bunches of roses, yellow and pink, large blooms and small, the big ones at the centre decorating a bowl of peaches and strands of grapes heaped high, and pink blooms gave the lobsters a glow of sweetness, the promise of white flesh. Somehow to bring rose gardens and the sea together was Frog art, and I saw the point of it that night, though as a rule I disparage bourgeois decorations of the plate. She'd poured chilled white wine into a jug to give it air and to get rid of 'bottle stench', *l'odeur de la bouteille* she called it, she knows a thing or two, and the bread was warm and crisp and the butter just the right temperature for spreading. As for the mayonnaise, it was perfection, made with lemon juice and not with 'orrid vinegar, and with a *soupçon* of English mustard. *Bon appetit*, she said when we sat down and she helped us to salad. Afterwards I volunteered to make the coffee and made a strong brew. I wanted to stay awake until the next day, until my shot was fired.

I was, you can imagine, a fraudulent lover that night. One gives much away when making love, and I had to be careful not accidentally to inform Annie of terror, to keep all knowledge of tomorrow to myself. When I'd practice-fired the gun from my window I'd aimed high and had worked out as best I could the trajectory of the bullet to make it land in the trees. I'd been startled by the pull of the gun, the jerk which went like a shock up my arm, all the way up to my shoulder. I thought I might see the bullet leave the barrel but heard only the explosion, and then the echo of it. And that echo was a new noise for me and I kept on listening for it. How could I be sure that the tremors I'd felt in my arm would not repeat themselves when I embraced Annie, that the tension of touch when I became one with her would not enter her like a bacillus to infect her? I guarded myself from all this, and responded half-heartedly only to her loving approach. When she miaowed the loudest I fired my lust into her. That was nice.

The next morning, thank God, was uneventful. Lothar rose late and Annie, as I'd expected, was much her old self once more. There were several screams of *café, mes enfants*, like Louise spreading corn in the yard and calling the chickens, and I listened becalmed to Annie's and Lothar's chirping. I was remote from their conversation and listened only from afar. When finally I came out of my room I wore my jacket and stooped the way Mama had always deplored, so as not to show the bulge of the gun. The palms of my hands were moist, I used the hot mug of coffee to dry them, but the heat, I could feel, shot up to my brow, and I was frightened Annie might suspect a fever. Bonzo gave fortitude. He reminded me how hot he'd been at times on the car radiator and never lost his cool. That helped.

I'd not been able to work that day. I'd had it in mind to sort out my papers, to write several letters I owed, one to Schloss to direct him not to send any more money for the time being, but I knew I'd not accomplish anything that day and made no

183

attempt to set about these tasks. I wished I had someone to talk to, such as the warder who plays cards with the prisoner, or noughts and crosses, the one who will, in an hour or so, lead the condemned to the gallows. Those fellows are the only ones left in the end to guide you on your path. I wanted to see butterflies rise from my stomach, to emerge from the chrysalis of fear, to flutter before my eyes, colour and sensuous wings, I wanted the sunlight to bleach everything into a haze of light. Then Annie summoned us to lunch.

I was never so deft at eating trout. My concentration was fixed on picking the fish. I was glad there was an excuse for lack of conversation, there always is when fish with bones are served. I refused wine, fish need water I said, one of Mama's sayings, though I almost choked when Annie announced they were off that afternoon to visit the grave of Karl Marx at Highgate Cemetery. She patted my back because she thought I'd swallowed a bone, before going off to make the coffee.

Ten more minutes, four to make coffee, the water will take that long to boil, and whilst she waits she'll put some *petits fours* on a plate, and four more minutes in which she pours and we drink our cupfuls, then she'll be off to repair her face before going out. *Encore?* she asked Lothar, and he held his cup up like a good boy for a second helping. Then off she went. As he raised the cup to his lips I pulled out the gun, took aim and made some sound to make him look up. I wanted to give him the chance to make peace with his maker, that's if he wanted to do so. For a moment he didn't know what was happening - something, quite frankly, I hadn't reckoned on, for I wanted him to cry out at once to make Annie come back to witness what I was doing. That, after all, was the chief purpose of killing him, her watching him die.

'What are you doing with that?' he asked. 'That's my gun.'
'Yeah!'

To say that I had to widen my mouth and show my teeth. It must have looked like a grin, which amused me so much that I started to giggle.

'Don't play the fool with that thing in your hand.'

'I'm going to fire as soon as Annie comes in,' I told him, and wanted to add, 'to take you to the cemetery', but refrained from making a joke in bad taste at a moment like that. There he sat like El Greco's *Apotheosis of Jesus*, his head tilted to one side, his eyes staring at me, not a sound coming from him. Most likely his words had rattled to a standstill and were stuck in his throat. He tried to pull himself up on the sides of his chair, but I wouldn't allow this and stopped him by raising the gun, just a little gesture to show him I meant business, and that stopped him in his tracks.

Annie came in all bright and chic. She saw at once what I was about and screamed at me. 'Vot are you doing viz that gun, Fabrice? Put it down, my pet, please.' She stamped her foot on the ground and repeated 'at once' several times in rising crescendo.

Enough, I thought, of prolonging Lothar's exit. If I don't watch out she'll sit on his lap and shield him, then what shall I do? So I fired the gun, what a good gun it was. My finger felt cold as death. I hit Lothar on the left of the chest, two shots I fired, they landed bang on target. That was well done.

When it was all over it was my turn to sit still. I watched Annie squirm in anguish. 'Vot 'ave you done? *Lotharre* is dead! Why did you kill 'im? She put her arms round him, and tried to heave him up to see where he'd been hit. She put her cheek to his mouth to feel if there was any breath still coming from him, and when she saw there was none she let go of him, gently releasing her arm and said, 'Oh, my pet, oh my sweet pet, vot 'ave you done?'

She came up to me and repeated endearing words and stroked the back of my head, and then she embraced me. She wanted, I know, to kiss me but held back for a moment out of deference to the dead. I thought I'd felt moisture on my cheeks, and that was confirmed when I heard her sob and I tried to console her as best I could. I must say my heart wasn't in it. I felt pleased I'd concluded what I'd set out to do, strangely elated as I feel at times when I finish a poem as well as having started it, it's on account of that terrible craving we have for a beginning and

185

end. I detest that craving, Madame, you know that, that's why I won't let you pass away, and that's why I keep you up in the air or hide you in distant lands.

I'm busy now. In a few minutes the fuzz will come to take me away. I'll see you later, Maman. By the way, you must tell about Tibet. You've not spoken to me about your trip to Lhasa since your return.

* * *

Annie had rung me at the museum and asked me to come at once.

'I heard his laughter, this manic laughter, so loud I came out of the bedroom still holding my lipstick to see what was happening.'

That's what Annie told me when I arrived.

'Fabrice is very unwell.'

Fabrice, she said, had been talking a great deal about our Viennese cousin, Lothar, and about some goats he had shot in the Austrian Alps. The name of Kramer, the Belsen commandant, had come up several times, and Annie said she had tried to listen to Fabrice, and to make sense of what he was saying, but with little success. 'Fabrice', she said, 'loves scapegoats. They suddenly appear, and they stay for some time until, I believe, he changes their names,' she laughed, 'so you're never quite certain exactly where you are. But now he's calm, quite calm. Wherever did he get hold of that gun?'

She was glad, I could tell, that I had come, and to hand over Fabrice into my care. I could see what state he was in, that he needed treatment, and I made the arrangements as I had done before, and then waited with him in his room for the ambulance to arrive.

Annie had found him drooped in his chair, a gun at his side, and then he had started to crawl about on all fours, making weird noises. He even tried to climb the wall and broke a vase and a small table he tried to stand on. Then he fell over and got up and was calm.

186

Annie left us alone in the room. She said she didn't want to watch Fabrice being taken away, though he tried to make his exit a jolly occasion. There was much life in his step as he sauntered downstairs between the two nurses who had come to fetch him. 'I wish Bonzo were here,' he said. 'I'd like to give him a lick and a chew.'

His instructions, called out to me as he finally mounted the ambulance, to eat plenty of iron, amused the little crowd which had gathered to watch Fabrice being taken away. I remained on the same spot as the vehicle drove off, and was suddenly aware that people were staring at me, and they continued to do so for another minute or two before dispersing. It was not until someone remarked that this was as good as the illusionist they had recently seen at the circus that I realized that my likeness to Fabrice had aroused their interest to stay behind after the ambulance had driven off. Both of us had worn dark coats that day, and they had seen me disappear into the ambulance and then reappear with a bundle of books under my arm. However, I was not prepared to give an explanation to anyone, and turned to walk to my place round the corner. And then, as soon as I got home, I started to read my brother's journals for the first time.

Am I expected, at the end, to verify or to deny, to set the record straight, as they say, some of the events Fabrice has decribed? Did Lothar actually shoot Kramer's goats, is Maman dead, is Lothar dead, and Alban? I refuse to answer any of these questions. As far as Fabrice is concerned he has told us the truth. At times I have felt he has left me out of much of his thinking, far more than I should have done had I written the journals, and if he had done the editing he would have been too impish not to have put his nose in at places which in fact he would have had no right to do. But then that's easy enough for me to say as the elder brother, twins though we may be, and identical at that. I am glad of the extraordinary discrepancies I found, for they clearly spell out our separateness, which has made me find that evasive privacy I have been seeking all my

187

life. Fabrice is no shadow of me, nor am I his shadow. That I can now clearly state. It will save me from being dragged any more into his wilderness, where so often he gets hopelessly lost, where I followed him at times to be there to protect him, with the result that I too got lost. I shan't allow him in future to play his tricks on me, to seduce me and suck me into his strange world.

As I said at the beginning, Fabrice knows how to converge. That's how he stays in touch, he is never far away and can appear at any moment and stand next to you. I once found him on Hampstead Heath, where I had gone to take a stroll with a friend from the museum. He had come out of hospital that day and on his way home to his room he had decided to go shopping. He was carrying a new handsome rucksack on his back and was dressed in a green suit made of sturdy material, and good boots. 'I'm off to the mountains,' he said, and then he offered me a match. 'Eat only the head. The sulphur tastes like hell!'

Then he laughed and went on his way.

Somewhere, very soon, we'll see each other again. I'll not have to wait long.